Sarrasine

Sarrasine

and

A Passion in the Desert

Honoré de Balzac

Translated by David Carter

ET REMOTISSIMA PROPE

Hesperus Classics

Hesperus Classics
Published by Hesperus Press Limited
4 Rickett Street, London sw6 1ru
www.hesperuspress.com

First published in *Revue de Paris* in 1830
First published by Hesperus Press Limited, 2007

Foreword © Kate Pullinger, 2007
Introduction and English language translation © David Carter, 2007

Designed and typeset by Fraser Muggeridge studio
Printed in Jordan by Jordan National Press

isbn: 1-84391-151-5
isbn13: 978-1-84391-151-7

CONTENTS

FOREWORD

Honoré de Balzac was possessed by hypergraphia for most of his days – at least that's my theory. Dead by the age of sixty-one, he nonetheless produced close to one hundred novels, as well as many short stories and plays, as well as essays and journalism. It is said that he usually spent sixteen hours a day writing, consuming upwards of 300 cups of coffee during that time (that's one cup of coffee every three minutes). I picture a pale writer hunched over an enormous ream of paper, a coffee-drip, hospital-style, suspended overhead: perfect conditions for one in the grip of a nineteenth-century writing fever.

Balzac's reputation as a writer rests on the detailed realism he brought to literature, his fictive gaze focused on the lives of the petite bourgeoisie, inspiring Proust and de Maupassant among many others. Both the stories in this volume were published around the same time, 1830, in a group of short novels and stories Balzac named *Scènes de la vie privée* ('Scenes from Private Life'); later this series developed into what by the end of that decade he began calling the *Comédie humaine*, a vastly ambitious project in which Balzac hoped to transcribe the whole of contemporary society. Hence, the need for coffee.

But the two stories here, *Sarrasine* and *A Passion in the Desert*, are very different from the work for which Balzac is revered: *Sarrasine* is a kind of gorgeous urban myth, while *A Passion in the Desert* is an orientalist fable. Both stories are lush and over-ripe, heavily scented and hugely sensual, and in both tales true love is ultimately – murderously – thwarted.

'"This show is frightening!" she exclaimed.' So begins *A Passion in the Desert*, and we embark on a story within a story, a device familiar to readers of Balzac and common to both these stories – the first person narrator recounting a story they themselves have been told to a lovely and, it must be said, slightly credulous, young woman whose main role is to look at the narrator 'in amazement'.

Napoleon had led his great expedition into Egypt at the turn of the century, and all of Europe was enthralled by news of his discoveries; the old Provençal soldier who tells his tale to the narrator in *A Passion in the Desert* (who in turn tells the tale to his astonished friend) was captured by Arabs in Upper Egypt.

The soldier escapes and takes flight into the desert where he is soon lost. Sheltering in a cave for the night (Balzac's desert is a dream desert, a place of endless sand, oases, palm trees, and, at night, a star-filled oriental sky), the soldier wakes up and discovers he is not alone; there is a panther, a *'petite maitresse'* possessed of a kind of weary exotic oriental *hauteur,* sleeping beside him. Will she kill him before he kills her? One imagines Flaubert reading this story en route to the brothels of the Nile, where he elaborated upon and then made his own this particular view of eastern femininity.

The novella *Sarrasine* is a tale of gothic glamour, depicting European culture at its most corrupt, like Edgar Allan Poe with lashings of lust and face paint. The de Lanty family, wealthy, good-looking and otherwise blessed, has a terrible secret: what is the true identity of the decrepit old man, who 'has the smell of the cemetery about him', is hideous to behold, and frequents their sophisticated house parties like a ghost? The narrator is privy to this secret, and his guest at the party, a young marquise 'whose figure was full and vivacious in its beauty' is desperate to hear it. But the story of the sculptor Ernest-Jean Sarrasine and the phantasmagorical La Zambinella is too much: the

Cardinal is a murderer, society a haven for aristocrats with too much money and too much time on their hands whose silly tricks result in death and despair. The narrator's tale is based on hearsay and rumour and myth, a tale of love gone bad, morals gone astray, set in a world where nothing is as it first seems.

The theorist Roland Barthes' book *S/Z* is entirely devoted to a detailed semiotic examination of *Sarrasine*. I first came across the story not through Barthes (however much I'd love to claim the contrary) but at the beginning of the 1990s when the English theatre company Gloria created a music theatre piece adapted from the text by the writer and director Neil Bartlett and the composer Nicolas Bloomfield, a production redolent with faded stage make-up, torn costumes and decaying sets. The story of the sculptor who falls desperately in love with the opera singer he thinks is a woman, and fears is a man, but who turns out to be neither was conveyed most vividly, and Sarrasine's desperate imprecation when he discovers La Zambinella's duplicity – '*To love and be loved* are from now on words devoid of any meaning for me... No more love! I am dead to all pleasure, to all human emotions' – ring in my ears still. The debased glamour of the novella was filtered through gorgeous operatic arias that depict the castrato who, like his ill-fated suitor, dares to believe for a few moments that he will be loved, after all, anyway.

The last European castrato, Alessandro Moreschi, died in 1922, and there remain only a few low-quality recordings of his voice – high, strange, and, there is no other word for it, unearthly. But the castrato lives on to this day in literature and film and in *Sarrasine* he lives on quite literally, the one-hundred-year-old oddity, the family shame who also created the family fortune. The narrator thinks the moral of the story is one of progress; the castrati are dying off, and 'they don't make wretched creatures like that any more'. But the marquise knows better; the city is a cruel and terrible place, 'crime and infamy have the right of refuge there'. Love does not conquer all and some secrets are secret for good reason.

– Kate Pullinger, 2007

INTRODUCTION

One of the first writers to perceive that Balzac's stories *Sarrasine* and *A Passion in the Desert* shared the common theme of unconventional love, with more than a hint of perversion, was the Baroness Aurore Duprès, who herself shocked Parisian society by challenging its notions of sexual identity through appearing dressed as a man and changing her name to George Sand. In a letter of 7th March 1831, she pointed out that Balzac's fame at that time depended on stories about the love of a soldier for a tigress (sic) and of an artist for a castrato.

Hitherto Balzac had published several novels under pseudonyms, a satirical piece called *The Physiology of Marriage*, the historical novel *The Last of the Chouans, or Brittany in 1880*, a series of short pieces called *Scenes from Private Life*, and some other short works and fragments.

Apart from the aspects of the stories stressed by Sand, the works also have other points of similarity. Both use the device of a story within a story, and in both cases the narrator tells his story to impress a beautiful woman; in *Sarrasine* the narrator is more obviously determined to seduce his female companion. Both ladies are in a vulnerable state of mind: the one in *Sarrasine* is disturbed at the sight of a cadaverous old man at a society function and seeks from the narrator the story behind his strange association with the wealthy de Lanty family; in *A Passion in the Desert* the lady is anxious and incredulous after watching the performance of an animal tamer, and seeks an explanation of how such intimacy between a man and a wild animal is possible. Interestingly, the lady in *Sarrasine* is also described as being 'under the spell of that timid curiosity that drives women to acquire dangerous emotions, to see chained-up tigers…'

For *Sarrasine* there are several interesting literary parallels with which it may be fruitfully compared. The very magazine in which both stories had been originally published, the *Revue de Paris*, had also published in recent years translations of some of the fantastic stories by the German Romantic writer E.T.A. Hoffmann (1776–1822), whose stories also show considerable interest in mysterious figures, often ugly old men, neurotic young men, Italian opera, and beautiful young women who are not what they seem. His famous story 'The Sandman' (1816) is about a young man who falls obsessively in love with a young 'woman' who, as everybody else already knows, is an automaton (the basis of the ballet *Coppélia*, 1870, by Léo Délibes). In Hoffmann's story 'Don Juan' (1819) the protagonist falls in love with the prima donna in a production of Mozart's *Don Giovanni*. At the height of his obsession she appears in a ghostlike form in his box at the opera.

There are several later works with which *Sarrasine* also bears comparison. Oscar Wilde's *The Portrait of Dorian Gray* (1891) is also concerned with the unnatural pursuit of ideal beauty at the cost of one's humanity. And Thomas Mann's Gustav Aschenbach in *Death in Venice* (1912) is an artist who is drawn towards his own death by the godlike charms of a youth. But all is not what it seems: the authorities of the most serene cities cover up the presence of cholera and Mann reveals in telling detail that the youth may well be sick: he has some decaying teeth. More recently there is a close parallel in the play *M Butterfly* (1988) by David Henry Hwang, which is based on the true story of Bernard Boursicot's love for a 'female' Chinese opera singer, who was really a young man. The film version, directed by David Cronenberg, appeared in 1993. Balzac also provided some clear classical allusions in *Sarrasine*: to the legend of the sculptor Pygmalion, who fell in love with a beautiful statue, to the beautiful youth Adonis, and to the Lesbian poetess Sappho, as well as to the historical Antinous, favourite of the Emperor Hadrian. There is therefore a clear invitation to interpret the story in archetypal terms.

Perhaps the most notorious study of *Sarrasine* is that provided by Roland Barthes in his oddly titled work *S/Z* (1973). In this book he dissects the entire story, fragment by fragment. It is far too extensive to summarise in the present context. While many may feel that it distorts the meanings of the story, it does provide many interesting insights. For Barthes *Sarrasine* is a 'writerly' ('scriptible') text, meaning that it lends itself to complete dismemberment by a critic, who can feel free to impose on the text patterns of meaning, which often cannot be proved by citing other textual evidence, and do not need to be compatible with each other. This kind of text has, for Barthes, no final 'signifieds' but is an endless mesh of interrelated 'signifiers'. He divided the story into 581 small units (lexias) and applied to them 5 codes. These codes are not ranked in any way and several codes are often applied to the same lexia. They are referred to by the following adjectives: hermeneutic (relating to enigma and mystery); semic (associations evoked); symbolic (polarities and antitheses); proairetic (action and behaviour); and cultural (knowledge shared between text and reader). It must be said that Barthes produced a web of meanings and significances that would be unlikely to occur to the average intelligent reader during a careful reading of the text. It might be compared to interpreting all the pieces of a jigsaw puzzle individually without attempting to relate them to the total picture of which they are a part.

One should point out finally that the two stories are also different in various ways. Not the least is the fact that

Sarrasine depicts the profound shock of disillusionment at discovering that what was held to be reality is in fact artifice. The soldier in *A Passion in the Desert*, however, in his total isolation relishes the sensuality of the panther to the point that he knowingly identifies her with his mistress. While he gradually lets down his guard to become intimate with his 'mistress', he never forgets that she is a wild creature. There is no shattering of a dream, and he feels no regret at the end.

The translations are based on those editions known to contain Balzac's last amendments. While there are many uncertainties and variations, it has not been deemed wise to clutter this edition with them. A few interesting ambiguities have been commented on in the notes. The manuscript of *Sarrasine* has not been preserved, and each of the four early editions were subjected to alterations. It was first published in two parts in the *Revue de Paris* on the 21st and the 28th of November, 1830. It was republished in *Novels and Philosophical Tales* in 1831, where it had two chapters with headings. The present translation is based on the fourth edition in volume X of the *Comédie humaine*, published by Furne in 1844. *A Passion in the Desert* appeared as a 'Christmas Tale' in the *Revue de Paris* on the 24th of December, 1830. It was republished in volume XVI of the *Philosophical Studies* in 1837, and again in 1845 in volume IV of *Three Lovers*, with titled sections. The present translation is based on the text in volume VIII of the *Comédie humaine* published by Furne in 1846.

Some modifications have been made to Balzac's punctuation, bringing it more in line with current English usage. He uses semicolons, for example, more freely and fulfilling different functions than is common in English. His uses of ellipsis and italics have been retained.

Finally, full acknowledgements must be made of the generous help provided by friends in tracking down obscure meanings. They are Philip and Bénédicte Morris, Alan Miles and Allegra Carlton. Special thanks are also due to Katherine Venn for her ever-diligent editing.

– David Carter, 2007

Sarrasine

To Monsieur Charles de Bernard du Grail [1]

I was plunged into one of those profound daydreams that take possession of everyone, even a frivolous man, in the midst of the most tumultuous festivities. Midnight had just struck by the church of the Elysée-Bourbon. Seated in a window opening, and hidden by the wavelike folds of a curtain of shimmering material, I was able to contemplate in comfort the garden of the mansion where I was spending the evening. The trees, not perfectly covered with snow, stood out faintly against the greyish background formed by a cloudy sky, barely whitened by the moon. Seen amidst this fantastic atmosphere, they vaguely resembled ghosts poorly wrapped in their shrouds, a gigantic image of the famous 'dance of death'. Then, turning round to the other side, I was able to admire the dance of the living: a magnificent drawing room, with walls in silver and gold, with twinkling chandeliers, and gleaming with candles! It was teeming with the prettiest women in Paris, who were bustling about and flitting around. The richest, the most highly titled women were there, radiant, pompous, and dazzling you with their diamonds; they had flowers on their heads, on their bosoms, in their hair, sewn onto their dresses, or as garlands on their feet. Their light tremblings of joy and voluptuous steps caused the cotton and silk lace to ripple and the muslin around their delicate sides to roll up. Some looks, which were too vivacious, broke through all this here and there, eclipsing the lights and the fiery brilliance of the diamonds, and enlivened hearts that were already too passionate. You could also catch sight of ways of holding the head that were significant for lovers, and negative attitudes towards husbands. The raised voices of the gamblers at every unexpected throw, and the ringing sound of the pieces of gold, blended with the music and with the murmur of conversations. This crowd, which had been in-toxicated by everything the world had to offer in the way of seductions, was stupefied by the perfumed vapour and general drunkenness that was affecting their crazed imaginations. Thus, on my right, the sombre and silent image of death, and on my left the respectable bacchanalia of life; here cold dreary nature in mourning, there people enjoying themselves. And, on the borderline between these two disparate scenes, which, repeated a thousand times in various ways, make Paris the most entertaining city in the world and the most philosophical one, I was creating a mental blend, half pleasant, half funereal. With my left foot I was beating time, and the other, I believed, was in a coffin. In fact my leg was chilled by one of those drafts that freeze half your body, while the other half feels the muggy warmth of the drawing rooms, something that happens accidentally and quite frequently at balls.

'It can't be a very long time that Monsieur de Lanty[2] has owned this mansion.'

'Oh yes it is. It'll soon be ten years since the Maréchal de Carigliano[3] sold it to him…'

'Ah!'

'These people must have an enormous fortune?'

'Oh they must have.'

'What an event! And of such ostentatious luxury.'

'Do you think they're as rich as Monsieur de Nucingen or Monsieur de Gondreville?'[4]

'You don't know then?'

I moved my head forward and recognised the two people conversing as belonging to that strange class of people, who, in Paris, concern themselves exclusively with questions like *Why? How? Where is he from? Who are they? What is it? What has she done?* They started to talk in low voices and moved away to go and talk more at ease on some isolated sofa. Never had a more fruitful source opened up for those seeking mysteries.

Nobody knew what country the de Lanty family came from, nor from what business or form of despoiling, what piracy or inheritance a fortune estimated at several millions derived. All the members of this family spoke Italian, French, English and German sufficiently well to lead you to assume that they had had to stay for a long time among these various peoples. Were they Bohemians? Were they swindlers?

'Who cares if it was the devil himself,' said some young politicians, 'they entertain wonderfully well.'

'Had the Comte de Lanty robbed some kasbah, I would certainly marry his daughter,' a philosopher exclaimed.

Who would not marry Marianina, a young sixteen-year-old girl, whose beauty embodied the fabulous conceptions of oriental poets? Like the sultan's daughter in the story of 'The Magic Lamp',[5] she should have remained veiled. Her singing made the imperfect talents of the Malibrans, the Sontags and the Fodors[6] of this world pale. In them there has always been one dominant quality to the exclusion of the perfection of the whole, while Marianina knew how to combine to the same degree purity of sound, sensitivity, appropriateness of movement and intonation, soul and knowledge, correctness and feeling. This girl was the classic example of that secret poetry, the common link between all the arts, which always escapes those who seek it. Gentle and modest, educated and witty, nothing could eclipse Marianina except for her mother.

Have you ever met one of those women whose striking beauty defies the damaging effects of age, and who seem at thirty-six to be more desirable than they must have been fifteen years earlier? Their face is an impassioned soul, it sparkles; every feature gleams with intelligence, and every pore possesses a distinctive radiance, especially under lighting. Their appealing eyes attract, reject, speak or remain silent;

their way of acting is knowing but innocent; and their voice displays a melodious richness of the most coquettishly soft and gentle tones. When they praise someone it is well-founded on comparisons and flatters the most touchy sense of self-esteem. One movement of their eyebrows, the slightest glance of their eyes, the twitch of a lip, impose a kind of terror on those who make their lives and happiness dependent on them. Inexperienced in love and docile in speech, a young girl can let herself be seduced, but for these sort of women, a man must know, as M. de Jaucourt[7] did, not to cry out, when, while he is hiding at the back of a side room, the maid breaks two of his fingers in the door jamb. By loving powerful sirens don't you risk your life? And that's perhaps why we love them so passionately. Such a woman was the Comtesse de Lanty.

Filippo, Marianina's brother, had, like his sister, the marvellous beauty of the countess. To express it all in one word, this young man was the living image of Antinous,[8] with a skinnier figure. But how well those thin and delicate proportions combine with youthfulness, when there are also an olive complexion, vigorous eyebrows and the fire of velvet eyes that give promise of male passions and noble ideas for the future. If Filippo stayed in the hearts of all young girls as a classic type, then he remained just as much in the memories of all the mothers as the best match in Paris.

The beauty, fortune, minds and graces of these two children came solely from their mother. The Comte de Lanty was small, ugly and pockmarked, dark like a Spaniard, and as boring as a banker. He passed for a profound politician, perhaps because he rarely laughed, and was always quoting M. de Metternich[9] or Wellington.

This mysterious family had all the appeal of a poem by Lord Byron, the difficulties of which had been rendered in a different way by each member of high society: an ode in which every single verse was obscure and sublime. The reticence that M. and Mme de Lanty maintained about their origins, their past existence and their connections with the four corners of the world, was said not to have been a matter of surprise for a long time in Paris. In no other country perhaps is the axiom of Vespasian[10] better understood. There, even crown coins stained with blood or mud do not betray anything and mean everything. As long as high society can put a figure to your fortune, you are ranked among those sums of money that do not matter to you, and no one asks to see your documentary proof, for everyone knows how little it is worth. In a city where social problems are solved by algebraic equations, adventurers have excellent opportunities in their favour. Assuming that this family had been Bohemian in origin, it was so rich, so attractive, that high society could well have forgiven it for its little mysteries. But, unfortunately, the enigmatic history of the de Lanty household would arouse permanent curiosity, quite like that for the novels of Anne Radcliffe.[11]

Observers, those people who like to know in which shop you buy your candelabras, or who ask you how much the rent is if your apartment seems lovely to them, had noticed every now and then, in the middle of celebrations, concerts, balls and ordinary festivities given by the countess, the appearance of a strange person. It was a man. The first time he showed himself in the mansion was during a concert, where he seemed to have been attracted to the drawing room by the enchanting voice of Marianina.

'Since a moment ago, I feel cold,' a lady seated near the door said to another next to her.

The unknown man, who was standing near this woman, moved away.

'How strange! Now I'm warm,' said this woman after the stranger's departure. 'And you'll probably accuse me of being mad, but I don't know how I can avoid thinking that my neighbour, that man dressed in black who has just left us, caused this coldness.'

Soon the natural exaggeration among people in high society caused the birth and accumulation of the most amusing ideas, the strangest expressions and the most ridiculous stories about this mysterious person. Without being precisely a vampire, a ghoul, an artificial man, a type of Faust or Robin Hood,[12] he shared something, according to those people who were lovers of the fantastic, with all these anthropomorphic natures. There were to be found here and there some Germans who considered these ingenious mocking expressions of malicious Parisian gossip to be true. The stranger was simply an *old man*. Several of those young men, who are accustomed to decide every morning the future of Europe in a few elegant phrases, would have it that the unknown man was a great criminal, and possessor of an enormous fortune. Novelists recounted the life of this old man and gave you really strange details about the atrocities committed by him during the time he was in the service of the Prince of Mysore.[13] Some bankers, more positive people, introduced a specious tall story: 'Bah!' they said, shrugging their large shoulders in a movement expressing pity, 'This little man is a "Genoese head"'.[14]

'Sir, if you don't mind my asking, would you be so good as to explain to me what you mean by a "Genoese head"?'

'Sir, it is a man on whose life enormous capital funds are based, and it is on his good health no doubt that the revenue of this family depends.'

I remember having heard, at the home of Mme d'Espard, a hypnotist[15] prove by taking into account very specious historical factors, that this old man, when subjected to close scrutiny, was the famous Balsamo, known as Cagliostro.[16] According to this modern alchemist, the Sicilian adventurer had escaped death, and amused himself making gold for his grandchildren. Finally the bailiff de Ferrette[17] claimed to have identified this strange character as the Comte de Saint-Germain.[18] These stupid ideas expressed in a witty way, and with an air of mockery, which is nowadays characteristic of a society without beliefs, kept alive vague suspicions about the de Lanty household. Finally, by an unusual combination of circumstances, the members of this family justified the world's conjectures by behaving in quite a mysterious way with regard to this old man, whose life was in some way concealed from all investigations.

If this person crossed the threshold of the apartment that he was supposed to occupy in the de Lanty mansion, his appearance always caused a great sensation in the family. One would have said it was a highly important event. Fillipo, Marianina, Mme de Lanty and an old servant were the only ones who were privileged to help the unknown man to walk, get up and sit down. Each of them kept a watch on his smallest movements. It seemed that he was an enchanted being, on whom the happiness, life and fortune of all of them depended. Was it fear or affection? Society people could not discover any evidence that helped them to resolve the problem. Hidden away for whole months, deep in some unknown sanctuary, this familiar spirit came out suddenly in a furtive way, unexpectedly, and appeared in the middle of a drawing room, like those fairies of some former times who would descend from their flying dragons to come and disturb ceremonies to which they had not been invited. Only the most practised observers could then discern the anxiety of the masters of that home, who knew how to conceal their feelings with unusual skill. But sometimes, while dancing a quadrille, Marianina, who was too innocent, cast a look of terror at the old man whom she was watching among the groups of people. Or Filippo, sneaking through the crowd, would dash forward to join him, and stay beside him, tender and attentive, as if contact with human beings or the least breath would shatter this strange creature. The countess would try to approach him, without appearing to have had any intention of joining him, and then, adopting a manner and look imbued as much with servility as with tenderness, with submission as with despotism, she would say two or three words, to which the old man would almost always defer, and he would disappear, led, or rather it would be better to say taken away, by her. If Mme de Lanty was not there, the count would employ a thousand stratagems to reach him; but he had a manner of seeming to listen with difficulty, and he would treat him like a spoiled child whose mother listens to its tantrums or dreads its disobedience. Whenever any indiscreet people had unthinkingly ventured to question the Comte de Lanty, this cold, reserved man had never appeared to understand the questions put to him by these inquisitive people. Also, after many attempts, which were rendered futile by the cautious behaviour of all members of the family, no one tried to discover such a well-guarded secret. Those who spy on social gatherings, those who will swallow anything, and politicians had ended up, weary of battle, by not concerning themselves with this mystery anymore.

But at the same time there were perhaps in the midst of these resplendent drawing rooms some philosophers who, while having an ice or a sorbet, or placing their empty punch glass on a console table, would say to each other: 'I would not be surprised to learn that those people are crooks. That old man, who hides himself away and only appears at equinoxes or solstices, looks to me like a murderer…'

'Or a bankrupt…'

'It's almost the same thing. To destroy a man's wealth is sometimes worse than killing the man himself.'

'Sir, I bet twenty louis,[19] and it comes to forty for me.'

'My God sir! There's only thirty left on the table…'

'Ah well, you can see what a mixed company we're in here. You can't even gamble.'

'It's true. But it'll soon be six months since we last saw the Spirit. Do you believe he is a living being?'

'Ha! Ha! At the very most…'

These words were uttered near me by some strangers, who went away at the moment when I was summing up in one last thought my mixture of black and white reflections about life and death. My crazy imagination as much as my eyes contemplated each in turn, now the festivities, which had reached the highest point of their splendour, and now the sombre tableau of the gardens. I do not know how long I meditated on these two sides of the human coin, but suddenly the stifled laughter of a young woman woke me. I was left amazed at the appearance of the image that presented itself to my eyes. By one of the rarest freaks of nature, the thought dressed in semi-mourning, which was rolling around in my mind, had come out and stood before me, in person, alive. It had burst like Minerva from the head of Jupiter, big and strong; it was both a hundred and also twenty-two years old, it was alive and dead. Having escaped from his room, like a madman from his place of confinement, the little old man had undoubtedly slipped cleverly behind a row of people paying attention to the voice of Marianina, who was finishing the cavatina from *Tancredi*[20]. He seemed to have come out from under the ground, pushed up by some theatrical mechanism. Motionless and sombre, he stayed for a moment to look at the festivities, the murmur of which had perhaps reached his ears. His preoccupied state, almost somnambulistic, was so concentrated upon things that he was in the midst of people without seeing them. He had appeared suddenly without ceremony beside one of the most ravishing women in Paris, an elegant young dancer with a delicate figure, and with one of those faces as fresh as that of a child, white and pink, and so frail, so translucent, that it would seem that a man's glance must penetrate them as the rays of the sun pass though a clear sheet of glass. They were there, in front of me, the two of them, together, united and so close that the stranger crumpled the gauze dress, the garlands of flowers, the lightly combed-back hair and flowing waistband.

I had brought this young woman to Mme de Lanty's ball. As it was the first time for her to come to this house, I forgave her muffled laugh, but I waved to her in a kind of imperious way that completely dumbfounded her and made her show respect for her neighbour. She sat down near me. The old man did not want to leave this delightful creature, to whom, on a whim, he attached himself with that silent obstinacy, and without any apparent reason, that extremely old people are prone to, and makes them resemble children. To sit down next to the young woman he had to take a fold-up stool. His slightest movements were marked by that cold awkwardness, that stupid indecision that characterise the movements of a paralysed person. He settled down slowly onto his seat, cautiously, grumbling a few unintelligible words. His hoarse voice was like the noise made by a stone falling into a well. The young woman squeezed my hand firmly, as if she had tried to prevent herself from falling over a precipice, and she shuddered when that man, at whom she was looking, turned a pair of eyes, devoid of warmth, upon her, murky eyes that could only be compared to tarnished mother-of-pearl.

'I'm afraid,' she said, leaning towards my ear.

'It's alright to speak,' I replied. 'He can only hear with great difficulty.'

'You know him then?'

'Yes.'

So she became sufficiently bold enough to examine for a moment this creature for which there is no name in human language, a form without substance, a being without life, or life without action. She was under the spell of that timid curiosity that drives women to acquire dangerous emotions, to see chained-up tigers, to look at boas, frightening themselves at being separated by nothing but weak barriers. Although the little old man had a bent back like that of a daily labourer, you could notice easily that he must have been of ordinary size. His excessive thinness, the delicacy of his limbs proved that his proportions had always remained slender. He was wearing black silken pantaloons that fluttered around his emaciated thighs, forming folds like a veil that had been pulled down. An expert in anatomy would have recognised at once the symptoms of a horrible emaciation on seeing the small legs that had to support that strange body. You would have said that they were like two crossed bones on a grave. A feeling of profound horror of the man gripped your heart when your attention was fatally drawn to him, revealing the marks that decrepitude had etched on that frail machine. The stranger wore a white, gold-embroidered waistcoat, in an old-fashioned style, and his linen was dazzling white. Quite a rust-coloured jabot of English lace, the magnificence of which would have been envied by a queen, hung down in yellowish folds on his

13

chest, but on him this jabot was more like a rag than a decoration. In the middle of this jabot a diamond of incalculable worth sparkled like the sun. This outmoded luxury, this intrinsic and tasteless treasure made the figure of this strange being stand out the more. The frame was worthy of the portrait. That dark face was angular and hollow all over. The chin was hollow; the temples were hollow; and the eyes were lost in yellowish eye sockets. The jawbones, made prominent by their indescribable thinness, outlined cavities in the middle of each cheek. These bumps, illuminated somewhat by the lights, produced strange shadows and reflections that completely removed from the face all characteristics of a human face. And the years had caused the fine yellow skin of the face to stick to the bones so firmly that it was marked by a mass of wrinkles or circular effects, like the ripples in water that is disturbed by a child throwing a pebble, or crazed like a crack in a window pane, but always deep and as pressed together as the pages at the edge of a book. Some old men often present us with more hideous portraits, but what contributed most to lending the appearance of something created artificially to the spectre that had risen before us was that there was a red and white gleam about it. The eyebrows on its mask were lent a sheen by the light, which revealed a well-executed painting. Fortunately for those saddened by the view of so much that was ruined, his cadaverous skull was hidden by a blond wig, the countless curls of which betrayed a remarkable pretentiousness. Besides, the feminine vanity of this fantastic figure was already forcefully proclaimed by the golden rings hanging from his ears, by the rings with stunning precious stones that shone brilliantly on his ossified fingers, and by a watch chain that sparkled like the settings of a necklace on a woman's neck. Lastly, this kind of Japanese idol kept a permanent fixed expression of laughter on his bluish lips, a harsh mocking laughter, like that of a death's head. Silently, and as immobile as a statue, it exhaled the musky odour of the old clothes that the heirs of a duchess exhume from her drawers during an inventory. If the old man turned his eyes towards the gathering, it seemed that the movements of those eyeballs, which were incapable of reflecting a gleam of light, were carried out by some imperceptible device. And when the eyes stopped, anyone who was examining them would end up doubting if they had moved. What it was to see, beside these human remains, a young woman whose neck, arms and bodice were bare and white, whose figure was full and vivacious in its beauty, whose well-arranged hair on an alabaster forehead inspired love, whose eyes did not absorb light but emitted it, who was suave, fresh, and whose diaphanous curls and fragrant breath seemed too heavy, too harsh and too strong for this shade, for this man of dust! Ah, in my mind it was Death and Life, an imaginary arabesque, half a hideous chimera, and also divinely female due to the bodice.

'There are such marriages in the world, however, that are quite often fulfilled,' I said to myself.

'He has the smell of the cemetery about him,' exclaimed the horrified young woman, who grasped at me as though to assure herself, and whose tempestuous movements conveyed to me that she was very much afraid. 'It's a horrible sight,' she resumed. 'I couldn't bear staying there for a long time any more. If I look at him again, I'll believe that Death himself has come looking for me. But is he alive?'

She laid her hand on the freak with that boldness that women are capable of in the violence of their desires, but a cold sweat exuded from her pores, for as soon as she had touched the old man, she heard a cry like the sound of a rattle.

This sharp voice, if it was a voice, escaped from an almost withered gullet. Then this raucous sound was followed swiftly by the little cough of a child, convulsive and with an unusual tone. At this noise Marianina, Filippo and Mme de Lanty took a quick look at us, and their eyes seemed to flash. The young woman could have wished herself at the bottom of the Seine. She took my arm and led me towards a boudoir. Everyone, men and women, made way for us. Reaching the back of the apartments set aside for receptions, we entered a small semicircular side room. My female companion threw herself onto a couch, panting with terror, not knowing where she was.

'Madame, you are mad,' I said to her.

'But,' she continued after a moment's silence during which I was admiring her, 'is it my fault? Why does Madame de Lanty allow such ghosts to wander around her mansion?'

'Oh, come on,' I replied, 'You regard that little old man as a ghost.'

'Do be quiet,' she responded with that imposing and mocking manner that all women know well how to adopt when they want to be right. 'What a pretty boudoir!' she exclaimed looking around her. 'Blue satin is wonderfully effective as a wall-covering. Is it fresh? Oh, what a beautiful picture!' she added as she stood up and went and stood in front of a magnificently framed canvas.

We stayed for a moment contemplating this marvel, which seemed to have been produced by some supernatural brush. The picture represented Adonis stretched out upon a lion's skin. Furthermore, the lamp, hanging in the middle of the boudoir and contained in an alabaster vase, illuminated this canvas with a soft glow that allowed us to catch all the beautiful qualities of the painting.

'Does such a perfect being exist?' she asked me after having examined, not without a gentle smile of satisfaction, the exquisite elegance of the outlines, the pose, the colour, the hair, in fact everything.

'He's too beautiful for a man,' she added, after an inspection similar to that she would have conducted on a rival.

Oh, how I felt then those attacks of jealousy that a poet had vainly tried to make me believe in! The jealousy of engravings, of pictures, of statues, in which artists exaggerate human beauty, following the doctrine that leads them to idealise everything.

'It's a portrait,' I replied to her. 'It's by the talented artist Vien.[21] But that great painter never saw the original, and your admiration will be less keen perhaps when you learn that this nude study was based on a statue of a woman.'

'But who is it?'

I hesitated.

'I want to know,' she added sharply.

'I think,' I said to her, 'that this Adonis depicts... a relative of Madame de Lanty.'

I was grieved to see her plunged deeply into contemplation of that figure. She sat down in silence. I placed myself beside her and took her hand without her noticing. Forgotten for a portrait! At that moment the faint noise of the footsteps of a woman with a rustling dress resounded in the silence. We saw young Marianina come in, looking the more radiant for her innocent expression than for her grace and for having freshened up her appearance. Well, she was walking slowly, and, with maternal care and filial concern, she was holding on to the smartly dressed spectre, who had caused us to flee the music room. With a kind of anxiety she watched him slowly placing his weak feet. With considerable difficulty they arrived together at a hidden door in the wall-covering. Once there, Marianina knocked softly. Immediately there appeared, as if by magic, a big gaunt man, a kind of familiar spirit. After entrusting the old man to this mysterious guardian, the young child kissed the walking corpse respectfully, and her innocent caress had something of that graceful way of cuddling, the secret of which certain fortunate women possess.

'*Addio, addio!*' she said, with the nicest inflections to her young voice.

She even added a well executed melisma to the last syllable, but in a low voice, and as though to manifest the effusive feelings of her heart through a poetic expression. The old man, struck suddenly by some memory, stayed in the doorway of this secret little room. Then we heard, by virtue of the deep silence, the heavy sigh that came from his chest: he drew off the most beautiful of the rings, with which his skeletal fingers were loaded, and placed it at Marianina's bosom. The crazy young woman started to laugh, took the ring, slipped it under her glove onto one of her fingers, and dashed off swiftly towards the drawing room, where there resounded at that moment the prelude to a quadrille. She caught sight of us.

'Ah! You were there!' she said with a blush.

After having looked at us in an interrogating way, she ran to her dancing partner with the carefree exuberance of her age.

'What does it mean?' my young partner asked me. 'Is it her husband? I think I'm dreaming. Where am I?'

'You!' I replied. 'You, who are highly impassioned and who, understanding so well the most imperceptible emotions, know how to cultivate feelings in the heart of the most refined man, without ruining his name, without destroying him from the first day, you who have pity for the sorrows of the heart, and who combine the mind of a Parisian woman with a passionate soul worthy of Italy or Spain…'

She saw clearly that my language was marked by a bitter irony, and then, in a way that did not seem to be inadvertent, she interrupted me to say, 'Oh! You mould me to suit your own taste. It's an unusual kind of tyranny! You don't want me to be *myself*.'

'Oh! I don't want anything,' I exclaimed, appalled by her severe attitude. 'Is it true, at least, that you like to hear some accounts of those strong passions engendered in our hearts by those delightful women of the south?'

'Yes. Well?'

'Well, I shall come to your home tomorrow evening around nine o'clock, and reveal this mystery to you.'

'No,' she replied with a mischievous air, 'I want to hear about it straight away.'

'You have not yet given me the right to obey you by saying "I want…"'

'At this moment,' she replied, with a desperate coquettishness, 'I have the keenest desire to know this secret. Tomorrow, perhaps, I won't listen to you…'

She smiled, and we separated, she still as proud and hard, and me still as ridiculous at that moment as ever. She had the audacity to dance a waltz with a young aide-de-camp, and I remained by turns angry, sulky, admiring, loving and jealous.

'Till tomorrow,' she said to me at about two o'clock in the morning, when she left the ball.

'I shan't go,' I thought. 'And I'll give you up. You are more fickle, perhaps a thousand times more unpredictable, than I can imagine.'

The next day, we were in front of a good fire, in a small elegant drawing room, sitting together. She was on a small two-seater sofa and I on cushions, almost at her feet, and below her eye level. The street was silent. The lamp cast a soft light. It was one of those evenings that give delight to the soul, one of those moments that are never forgotten, one of those hours spent at peace and in desire, and the charm of which is later always cause for regret, even when we find ourselves happier. Who can erase the vivid trace of the first incitements of love?

'Come along,' she said, 'I'm listening.'

'But I dare not start. The adventure has some passages that are dangerous for the narrator. If I get enthusiastic about it, you will make me be silent.'

'Speak!'

'I obey.'

'Ernest-Jean Sarrasine was the only son of a prosecutor in Franche-Comté,[22] I started again after a pause. 'His father had obtained quite honestly an annuity of six to eight million livres,[23] a fortune for a practitioner, which, formerly, in the provinces, was regarded as enormous. Old Maître[24] Sarrasine, having only one child, did not want to neglect anything for his education. He hoped to make a magistrate of him, and to live long enough to see, in his old age, the grandson of Matthieu Sarrasine, a farm labourer in the Sainte-Dié[25] area, sitting in the high court and sleeping during a hearing, for the greater glory of parliament. But Heaven was not saving this joy for the prosecutor. The young Sarrasine, entrusted from a young age to the Jesuits, proved to be exceptionally unruly. He had the childhood of a talented man. He only wanted to study in a way that pleased him, and often rebelled and remained sometimes for hours on end deep in vague meditations, occupied at times in looking at his friends when they were playing, and at other times imagining to himself the heroes of Homer. Then, if he

20

managed to amuse himself, he bore an extraordinary fervour in his eyes. When some conflict arose between him and a friend, the struggle would rarely finish without blood being spilt. If he was the weaker he would bite. By turns active or passive, without any special aptitude or very much intelligence, his odd character made him feared by his teachers as much as by his friends. Instead of learning the rudiments of the Greek language, he would draw the reverend father who was explaining a passage of Thucydides to them, sketch the mathematics teacher, the prefect, the servants, and the examiner, and he daubed all the walls with shapeless sketches. Instead of singing praises to the Lord in church, he amused himself, during the services, by tearing a bench to pieces, or, when he had stolen some piece of wood, he would sculpt some kind of figure of a saint. If he did not have any wood, stone or pencil, he would convey his ideas with some crumbs of bread. Whether he copied the characters in the pictures that decorated the chancel, or whether he improvised, he would always leave on his seat some crude sketches, the licentious nature of which drove the youngest fathers to despair, and the malicious ones claimed that the old Jesuits smiled at them. Finally, if one is to believe the college chronicle, he was expelled, for having, while awaiting his turn in the confessional one Good Friday, sculpted a large piece of wood in the image of Christ. The impious detail engraved on this statue was too extreme for the artist not to bring some punishment on himself. Had he not had the audacity to place this rather cynical figure high up on the tabernacle!

'Sarrasine came to seek refuge in Paris against the threats of his father's curse. Having one of those strong wills that know no obstacles he obeyed the dictates of his genius and joined the studio of Bouchardon.[26] He used to work all day, and

21

in the evening he would go and beg to support himself. Bouchardon, amazed at the progress and intelligence of the young artist, soon sensed the destitution in which his pupil found himself. He helped him, became fond of him, and treated him as his own child. Then, when Sarrasine's genius was revealed by one of those works in which future talent struggles against the turmoil of youth, the generous Bouchardon tried to reinstate him in the good graces of the old prosecutor. Before the authority of the famous sculptor, the paternal fury abated. The whole of Besançon[27] was pleased to have brought a future great man into the world. In the first moment of ecstasy into which he was plunged by his flattered vanity, the miserly practitioner enabled him to look his best in society. The long and arduous studies required for sculpture subdued for a long time Sarrasine's impetuous nature and wild genius. Bouchardon, anticipating the violence with which passion might be unleashed in this young soul, perhaps as vigorously imbued as that of Michelangelo, stifled his energy under continuous work. He managed to confine Sarrasine's amazing enthusiasm within reasonable bounds, by forbidding him to work, by suggesting some forms of recreation when he noticed that he was overcome by some furious thought, or by entrusting him with some important tasks, at that moment when he was about to give himself up to dissipation. But, with this passionate soul, gentleness was always the most powerful of weapons, and the master only exerted authority over his pupil through stimulating gratitude by his fatherly kindness.

'At the age of twenty-two, Sarrasine was forcibly withdrawn from the beneficial influence that Bouchardon exerted on his lifestyle and habits. He was able to bear the sufferings of his genius when he won the sculpture prize established by the

Marquis de Marigny, the brother of Madame de Pompadour,[28] who did so much for the arts. Diderot[29] extolled the statue by the pupil of Bouchardon as a masterpiece. It was not without deep sorrow that the king's sculptor watched a young man leave for Italy, whom he had, on principle, kept in profound ignorance of the facts of life. Sarrasine had been Bouchardon's dining partner for six years. He was fanatical about his art, as Canova[30] has been since then. He got up at dawn, went into the studio and did not leave it again until night-time, and lived with his muse. If he went to the Comédie-Française,[31] he was taken there by his master. He felt so embarrassed at Madame Geoffrin's[31] and in the high society into which Bouchardon tried to introduce him that he preferred to stay alone, and renounced the pleasures of that licentious era. He had no other mistress but Sculpture and Clotilde,[33] one of the stars of the Opera. But this intrigue did not last. Sarrasine was sufficiently ugly, always badly dressed, and by nature so easy-going, so poorly organised in his private life, that the famous nymph, fearing some disaster, soon made the sculptor return to his love of the arts. Sophie Arnould[34] has uttered some witty remark or other on the topic. She was surprised, I believe, that her friend had been able to triumph over statues.

'Sarrasine left for Italy in 1758. During the voyage, his fervent imagination was fired under a copper-coloured sky and at the prospect of the marvellous monuments that are scattered throughout the country of the Arts. He admired the statues, the frescoes, the paintings, and, full of the wish to emulate, he arrived in Rome racked by the desire to inscribe his name amongst the names of Michelangelo and Bouchardon. Also, during the first days, he divided his time between working in a studio and studying the works of art that are so plentiful in Rome. He had already spent two weeks in that state of ecstasy that takes hold of the imagination of all young people at the sight of those supreme ruins, when, one evening, he went into the *Argentina* theatre,[35] in front of which a large crowd was flocking together. He enquired about the reason for this crowd and the people replied by uttering two names: Zambinella! Jomelli![36] He enters and sits in the stalls,[37] pressed up against two priests of considerable size, but quite fortunately he was seated near the stage. The curtain rose. For the first time in his life he heard that music, the delightful qualities of which Monsieur Jean-Jacques Rousseau[38] had praised to him so eloquently during one of the soirées of Baron d'Holbach.[39] The senses of the young sculptor were, so to speak, lubricated by Jomelli's sublimely harmonious accentuation. The languorous eccentricities of those skilfully blended Italian voices plunged him into a delightful ecstasy. He stayed speechless, motionless, not even feeling himself pressed against by the two priests. His soul entered into his ears and eyes. He believed he could hear through every pore. Suddenly applause, which caused the auditorium to resound, greeted the entrance onto the stage of the prima donna. She advanced coquettishly to the forestage, and greeted the public with infinite grace. The lights, the enthusiasm of a whole group of people, the illusion of the stage, the glamour of a costume, which, in that period, was quite inviting, all conspired together in this woman's favour. Sarrasine uttered cries of delight. He was admiring at that moment an ideal beauty, the perfect forms of which he had hitherto sought here and there in nature, requiring of a model, often of the lowest type, the curves of a fully developed leg, of another the shape of the bosom, from that one her white shoulders, and finally taking the neck of a young girl, the hands of this woman, and the shiny knees of this little boy,[40] without ever encountering beneath the cold skies of Paris the rich and exquisite creations of ancient Greece. Zambinella revealed to him those exquisite proportions of the female being that are so passionately desired, combined together in a really living and subtle way, and of which a sculptor is, at the same time, the severest and the most impassioned judge. The mouth was expressive, the eyes full of love, and the complexion of a dazzling whiteness. And one must combine with these details, which would have delighted a painter, all the wonders of the Venuses revered and rendered by the chisels of the Greeks. The artist could not stop admiring the inimitable elegance with which the arms were attached to the bust, the magnificent curve of the neck, the gracefully drawn lines of the eyebrows, of the nose, and then the perfect oval of the face, the purity of its clear outline, and the effect of the thick curved eyelashes, which ended in large voluptuous eyelids. It was more than a woman, it was a masterpiece! He found himself in that unhoped-for condition of love that would delight all men, and with qualities of beauty worthy to satisfy any critic.

'Sarrasine devoured with his eyes the statue of Pygmalion[41] that had come down from its pedestal for him. When Zambinella sang, there was a furore. The artist remained cool. Then he sensed a fire that suddenly sparkled in the depths of his intimate being, what one calls the heart, for want of a better word! He did not applaud, he said nothing, but experienced a mad impulse, a kind of frenzy, which only disturbs us at that age when desire has something terrible and diabolical about it. Sarrasine wanted to dash onto the stage and take hold of this woman. His strength, increased a hundredfold by a mental depression that it was impossible to explain, since these phenomena take place in a sphere inaccessible to human observation, tended to project itself with a distressing violence. To see him, you would have said he was a cold and stupid man. Fame, knowledge, the future, existence and his crowning achievements all faded. "To be loved by her, or die," was the sentence that Sarrasine imposed on himself. He was so completely intoxicated that he no longer saw the auditorium, the audience, the performers, and no longer heard the music. What was better, there was no distance between him and Zambinella; he possessed her; his eyes, fastened on her, took possession of her. An almost diabolical power enabled him to feel the breath of that voice, to breathe in the fragrant powder with which her hair was impregnated, to see the surfaces of that face, to count the blue veins in it that added subtle detail to its satin skin. Finally that agile voice, fresh and with a silvery tone, as supple as a thread, given form by the slightest breath of air, which winds and unwinds it, develops and disperses it, that voice struck his soul so sharply that more than once he let out involuntary cries, torn from him by those spasms of pleasure that are too rarely provided by the human passions.

'Soon he was compelled to leave the theatre. His trembling legs were almost refusing to support him. He was shattered, weak like a tense man who has given himself up to some dreadful fit of anger. He had had so much pleasure, or perhaps he had suffered so much, that his life had drained away like water from a vase that has been hit and knocked over. He felt a void inside him, a total collapse similar to those apathetic states that cause convalescents to despair of getting over a bad illness. Overcome by an inexplicable sadness, he went to sit on the steps of a church. There, with his back leaning against a column, he lost himself in meditation, which was confused like a dream. This passion had devastated him.

'On returning to where he was staying, he fell into one of those paroxysms of activity that reveal to us the presence of new principles in our existence. A prey to that first fever of love, which is devoted as much to pleasure as pain, he wanted to stave off his impatience and his delirium by drawing Zambinella from memory. It was a sort of practical meditation. On one such a sheet, Zambinella was in that posture, calm and cool in appearance, of which Raphael, Giorgione[42] and all the painters were fond. On another, she was turning her head sensitively while completing a melisma, and it seemed that she was listening to herself. Sarrasine made pencil sketches of his mistress in all kinds of poses: without a veil; seated; standing; lying down; either innocent or amorous; fulfilling, thanks to the frenzied work of his pencils, all the changing ideas that assail our imagination when we think deeply about a mistress. But his intense thoughts went further than drawing. He could see Zambinella, he talked to her, begged her, spent a thousand years of life and happiness with her, putting her in all imaginable situations, rehearsing, so to speak, the future with her.

'The next day he sent his servant to rent a box close to the stage for him for the whole season. Then, like all young people with a strong spirit, he exaggerated to himself the difficulties of his undertaking, and provided himself, as a first attempt to nourish his passion, the pleasure of being able to admire his mistress unimpeded. This golden age of love during which we enjoy our own feelings and in which we are almost self-sufficient in our happiness was not to last long for Sarrasine.

'But events took him by surprise when he was still under the charm of this spring-like hallucination, as naive as it was voluptuous. For about a week he lived out a whole life, busy in the morning kneading the clay, with the help of which he managed to make a copy of Zambinella, in spite of the veils, the petticoats, the corsets and the knots of ribbons that hid her from him. In the evening, settled early in his box, alone, lying on a sofa, he created for himself, like a Turk intoxicated on opium, a state of pleasure that was as inspiring and as extravagant as he could wish. At first he gradually familiarised himself with the excessively vivacious emotions conveyed to him by the singing of his mistress. Then he learned to control his eyes in looking at her, and he finally managed to contemplate her without fearing the explosion of suppressed fury, with which his soul had been filled on that first day. His passion became more profound as it became calmer. Besides, the unsociable sculptor did not allow his solitude, peopled with images and adorned with fantasies of hope and full of happiness, to be disturbed by his friends. He loved so strongly and so naively, that he had to submit to the innocent scruples with which we are assailed when we fall in love for the first time. In starting to perceive that it would be necessary to act soon, to start scheming, to ask where Zambinella lived, to know if she had a mother, an uncle, a tutor, a family, and finally in thinking of ways of seeing her, of talking to her, he felt his heart swell so much at such ambitious ideas, that he put off his cares to the following day, as happy with his physical sufferings as with his intellectual pleasures.'

'But,' said Mme de Rochefide, interrupting me, 'I see no sign yet of Marianina nor her little old man.'

'You only have eyes for him,' I exclaimed impatiently, like an author, for whom one destroys the effect of his *coup de théâtre*. 'For several days,' I continued after a pause, 'Sarrasine had gone faithfully to settle himself in his box, and his looks expressed so much love that his passion for Zambinella's voice would have been news all over Paris, if this adventure had

28

happened there, but in Italy, madame, at the theatre, everyone attends for his own reasons, with his passions, with some matter of the heart that avoids the spying eyeglasses.

'One evening the Frenchman noticed that people were laughing at him in the wings. It would have been difficult to know to what extremes he would have been driven if Zambinella had not come on the stage. She cast one of those eloquent looks at Sarrasine that often say very much more than women want. This look was a complete revelation. Sarrasine was loved! "If it's only a whim," he thought, already accusing his mistress of too much ardour, "she does not know what domination she will succumb to. Her whim will last, I hope, as long as I live." At this moment, three light knocks at the door of his box aroused the attention of the artist. He opened the door. An old woman entered with an air of mystery. "Young man," she said, "if you want to be happy, take care, wrap yourself in a cloak, pull a large hat down over your eyes, and then, at about ten o'clock in the evening, be at the via di Corso, in front of the Villa di Spagna."[43]

' "I'll be there," he replied, placing two louis into the wrinkled hand of the chaperone. He fled from his box, after having given a sign that he understood to Zambinella, who lowered her voluptuous eyelids shyly, like a woman who is happy at being understood at last. Then he ran back to his room, in order to add to his mode of dress all the seductive qualities that it could provide him with.

'As he left the theatre, a stranger stopped him by touching his arm. "Be careful, my French lord," the man said in his ear. "It's a matter of life or death. Cardinal Cicognara[44] is her[45] protector, and doesn't jest."

'If a demon had placed all the depths of hell between Sarrasine and Zambinella, he would at that moment have crossed them all in one bound. Like those immortal horses depicted by Homer, the sculptor's love had crossed immense distances in the twinkling of an eye. "Were Death to await me on leaving the house, I would go there even faster," he replied.

"*Poverino!*"[46] exclaimed the stranger as he disappeared. Aren't you only giving pleasure to a man in love, if you talk to him of danger? Never had Sarrasine's servant seen his master be so meticulous in dressing himself. His finest sword, a present from Bouchardon, the cravat that Clotilde had given him, his outfit in glittering material, his waistcoat of silvery wool, his golden snuff box, his valuable watches, all were taken out of the trunks, and he was adorned like a young girl who was to present herself before her first lover. At the appointed hour, intoxicated with love and seething with hope, Sarrasine, with his face wrapped in his coat, ran to the meeting place told him by the old woman. The chaperone was waiting. "You really took your time!" she said to him. "Come along." She led the Frenchman through several small lanes and stopped in front of a rather fine-looking palace. She knocked. The door opened. She took him though a labyrinth of stairs, galleries, and apartments that were only lit by the vague faint light of the moon, and arrived at a door, from between the cracks of which there leaked some bright light and from where there came the happy sounds of several voices. Sarrasine was suddenly dazzled, when, at a word from the old woman, he was admitted into the mysterious apartment, and found himself in a drawing room that was both brilliantly illuminated and sumptuously furnished, and in the middle of which stood a well-provisioned table, loaded with venerable wines, with pleasant decanters, the reddened facets of which were sparkling. He recognised the men and women singers from the theatre, mixed with charming women, all ready to start an orgy of artistes, which only awaited his arrival. Sarrasine suppressed a reaction of pique and put on a brave face. He had hoped for a poorly lit room, his mistress beside a fireplace, a jealous lover two paces away, matters of death and love, confidences exchanged in low voices, heart to heart, dangerous kisses, and faces so close that Zambinella's hair would have stroked his forehead, which would be charged with desire and burning with happiness. "Long live madness!" he exclaimed. "*Signori e belle donne*,[47] you will permit me to take my revenge later and show you my appreciation for the way you welcome a poor sculptor." After having received quite affectionate greetings from most of the people present, whom he knew by sight, he attempted to approach the large armchair on which Zambinella was nonchalantly lying. Oh! How his heart beat when he caught sight of her delicate foot, wearing those slippers, which, permit me to say madame, formerly used to lend women's feet such a pretty, such a voluptuous appearance, that I do not know how men could resist them. The white stockings pulled well up and with their green corners, the pointed slippers with high heels in the reign of Louis XV have perhaps contributed somewhat to the demoralisation of Europe and the clergy.'

'Somewhat!' said the marchioness. 'You haven't read about it?'

'Zambinella,' I continued, smiling, 'crossed her legs shamelessly, and shook playfully that which was above it, with the bearing of a duchess, suited well to her type of beauty, which was capricious and full of a certain engaging softness. She had taken off her theatre costume, and her body displayed a slender waist, emphasised by hooped petticoats and a satin dress embroidered with blue flowers. Her bosom, the treasures of which were concealed by luxuriously coquettish

31

lace, sparkled with whiteness. Her hair had been done a little like Madame du Barry,[48] her face, although dominated by a huge bonnet, only looked the sweeter, and the powder became her well. To see her thus was to adore her. She smiled gracefully at the sculptor. Sarrasine, completely dissatisfied at only being able to talk to her in front of witnesses, sat down politely next to her, and conversed with her about music, praising her for her prodigious talent; but his voice was trembling with love, fear and hope.

'"What are you afraid of?" Vitagliani, the most famous singer of the company, said to him. "Go on, you only have one rival to fear here." The tenor smiled silently. The smile was repeated on the lips of all the guests, whose attention had some hidden malice in it, which it was not intended a lover should notice. Making it public in this way was for Sarrasine like suddenly receiving a blow from a dagger to the heart. Although endowed with a certain strength of character, and though no circumstances could have any influence on his love, he had perhaps not yet thought that Zambinella was almost a courtesan, and that he could not at the same time have the pure delights that make the love of young girl such a delicious thing, and also the spirited fits of anger by which a woman of the theatre makes you pay for the treasures of her passion. He thought about it and resigned himself.

'Supper was served. Sarrasine and Zambinella sat down side by side without ceremony. During the first half of the feast, the performers kept things within moderation, and the sculptor was able to talk with the singer. He found her witty and sensitive, but she was surprisingly ignorant, and revealed herself to be weak-willed and superstitious. The delicacy of her constitution was also to be found in her understanding. When Vitagliani uncorked the first bottle of champagne,

Sarrasine could read in the eyes of the woman next to him quite acute fear at the small detonation produced by releasing the gas. The involuntary starting of her feminine constitution was interpreted by the amorous artist as a sign of excessive sensibility. The weakness charmed the Frenchman. There is so much protectiveness involved in a man's love! "You may use my strength as a shield!" Is this phrase not written at the end of all declarations of love? Sarrasine, too impassioned to utter a lot of compliments to the beautiful Italian woman, was, like all lovers, by turns serious, cheerful, or full of reverence. Although he appeared to listen to the guests, he did not hear a word of what they were saying, so much did he devote himself to the pleasure of being near to her, of lightly touching her hand, of serving her. He basked in a secret joy. Despite the eloquence of some shared looks, he was surprised by the reserve that Zambinella maintained towards him. She had been the first to press his foot and to annoy him with the mischievousness of an easygoing woman, but suddenly she had wrapped herself in modesty, like that of a young girl, after having heard Sarrasine talk about a trait that revealed the extreme violence of his character.

'When the supper turned into an orgy, the guests started to sing, inspired by the peralta and the pedro ximenès.[49] There were delightful duets, airs from Calabria, Spanish seguidillas, Neapolitan canzonette. There was exhilaration in everyone's eyes, in the music, in hearts and voices. There was a sudden overflowing of enchanting vivacity, a warm-hearted abandonment, an Italian good-natured mood, which nothing can give an idea of to those who know only gatherings in Paris, reunions in London, or social circles in Vienna. Jokes and expressions of love crossed to and fro like bullets in a battle, through the laughs, the impieties, and invocations to the Holy Virgin or *al*

Bambino.[50] Someone lay down on the sofa and started to go to sleep. A young girl was listening to someone declaiming, unaware of the fact that she was spilling Jerez[51] wine on the tablecloth. In the middle of this chaos, Zambinella, as though struck with terror, remained pensive. She refused to drink, ate perhaps a little too much, but a weakness for good food is, they say, charming in a woman. While admiring the modesty of his mistress, Sarrasine reflected seriously about the future. "She will doubtless want to get married," he said to himself. Then he abandoned himself to the delights of this marriage. His whole life did not seem to him to be long enough to exhaust the spring of happiness that he found deep in his soul. Vitagliani, his neighbour, poured him some drink so often, that at about three o'clock in the morning, without being completely drunk, Sarrasine was powerless against the frenzy he found himself in. In a moment of enthusiasm he swept the woman away into a kind of boudoir adjoining the drawing room, towards the door of which he had more than once turned his eyes. The Italian woman was armed with a dagger.

'"If you come near," she said, "I will be forced to plunge this weapon into your heart. Leave me! You would despise me. I have conceived too much respect for your character to give myself thus. I don't want to dishonour the feelings that you hold towards me."

'"Ah, ha!" said Sarrasine, "It's a bad way to extinguish a passion by only exciting it. Aren't you in fact already so corrupted that, with your experience in matters of the heart, you try to act like a young courtesan who arouses the emotions that she profits from?"

'"But today is Friday," she replied, alarmed by the Frenchman's violence. Sarrasine, who was not devout, found himself laughing. Zambinella leaped away like a young roe deer and dashed into the room where the feast was taking place. When Sarrasine appeared there, running after her, he was greeted by diabolical laughter. He noticed that Zambinella had fainted on a sofa. She was pale and seemed to be exhausted by the extraordinary effort that she had just made. Although Sarrasine knew little Italian, he heard his mistress saying in a low voice to Vitagliani: "But he'll kill me!" This strange scene completely confused the sculptor. He regained his reason. He remained motionless at first, but then he found the power of speech again, sat next to his mistress and protested his respect for her. He found the strength to sublimate his passion by making the most impassioned utterances to this woman. And to depict his love, he deployed a wealth of magic eloquence, that unofficial interpreter, which women rarely refuse to believe.

'At the moment when those first faint gleams of morning surprised the guests, a woman suggested going to Frascati.[52] Everyone greeted with lively cheering the idea of spending the morning at the Villa Ludovisi.[53] Vitagliani went down to hire some carriages. Sarrasine had the pleasure of driving Zambinella in a phaeton. Once they had left Rome, the gaiety, suppressed for a moment by the battle that everyone had fought against sleep, reawoke suddenly. Men and women alike seemed used to this strange life, to these continuous pleasures, to this ingrained habit of the artist, who makes life into a perpetual celebration, in which one laughs without reservation. The sculptor's companion was the only one who appeared worn out.

'"Are you ill?" Sarrasine said to her. "Would you rather go home?"

'"I'm not strong enough to put up with all these excesses," she replied. "I need to be cared for a lot; but near you I feel very well! Without you, I would not have stayed at that late supper. Spending the night like that makes me lose all my freshness."

'"You are so delicate," continued Sarrasine, looking at the sweet features of this charming creature.

'"Orgies ruin my voice."

'"Now that we are alone," exclaimed the artist, " and you do not need to fear any more the turmoil of my seething passions, tell me that you love me."

'"Why?" she replied, "What good will it do? I seemed pretty to you. But you are French, and your feelings will pass. Oh, you would not love me as I would like to be loved."

'"What!"

'"Without the goal of vulgar passion, purely. I detest men perhaps more than I hate women. I need to take refuge in friendship. The world is a desert for me. I am a cursed creature, condemned to understand happiness, to feel it, to desire it, and, like so many others, forced to see it flee from me all the time. Remember, my lord, that I will not have deceived you. I forbid you to love me. I can be a devoted friend to you, because I admire your strength and your character. I need a brother, a protector. Be all these things for me, but no more."

'"Not love you!" exclaimed Sarrasine, "But, my dear angel, you are my life, my happiness!"

'"If I were to tell you one thing, you would push me away from you in horror."

'"You coquette! Nothing can frighten me. Tell me that you will cost me my future, that in two months I will die, that I will be damned for having only embraced you." He embraced her despite the efforts that Zambinella made to escape from this passionate kiss. "Tell me that you are a demon, that you must have my fortune, my name, my fame. Do you want me to give up being a sculptor? Tell me."

'"What if I weren't a woman?" Zambinella asked timidly in a soft, silvery voice."

'"That's a good joke!" exclaimed Sarrasine. "Do you think you can deceive the eye of an artist? Have I not, for the last ten days, devoured, scrutinised and admired your perfections? Only a woman can have this plump, soft arm, this elegant figure. Ah! You want compliments!"

'She smiled sadly, and said in a murmur, "Such fatal beauty!" She raised her eyes to the sky. At that moment her look had such an indescribable expression of horror, which was so powerful, and so vivid, that Sarrasine started at it. "My French lord," she continued, "forget forever your moment of madness. I think highly of you, but, as for love, do not ask it of me. This feeling has been stifled in my heart. I have no heart!" she exclaimed, weeping. "The theatre in which you have seen me, that applause, that music, that fame, to which I have been condemned, that is my life. I have no other. In a few hours you will not see me with the same eyes. The woman that you love will be dead."

'The sculptor did not reply. He was racked by stifled rage that pressed on his heart. He could do nothing but look at this extraordinary woman with her inflamed eyes burning. That voice imbued with weakness, the attitude, manners and gestures of Zambinella, marked with sadness, melancholy and despondency, revived in his soul all the wealth of his passion. Every word stung him.

'At that moment they had arrived at Frascati. When the artist held out his arms to his mistress to help her step down, he felt that she was trembling all over. "What's wrong? You would be the death of me," he exclaimed, when he saw her turn pale, "if you suffered the least grief of which I was the cause, albeit innocently."

'"A snake!" she said, pointing out a grass snake, which was slithering along a ditch. "I'm afraid of those horrible creatures." Sarrasine squashed the head of the grass snake by stamping on it with his foot. "How can you be so courageous?" continued Zambinella, looking with obvious terror at the dead reptile. "So," said the artist, smiling, "can you dare to claim that you aren't a woman?"

'They rejoined their companions and walked in the woods of the Villa Ludovisi, which belonged to Cardinal Cicognara. That morning passed too quickly for the amorous sculptor, but it was crowded with incidents that revealed to him the coquettishness, the frailty, the delicate grace of this soul, which was weak and lacking in energy. She was a woman with sudden fears, irrational whims, instinctive emotions, groundless audacity, bravado and delightful subtlety of feelings. There was a moment when, venturing into the open countryside, the small company of merry singers saw from afar some men armed to the teeth and dressed in a way that was not reassuring. With the words "There are some bandits", everybody quickened their pace to gain the shelter of the surrounding wall of the cardinal's villa. At this critical moment, Sarrasine noticed by Zambinella's pallor that she did not have enough strength left to walk. He took her in his arms and ran along carrying her for some time. When he got close to a nearby vine, he put his mistress on the ground.

'"Explain to me," he said to her, "how this extreme weakness, which in another woman would be hideous, would displease me and the slightest evidence of which would almost be enough to extinguish my love, in you pleases me, charms me." He continued, "Oh! How much I love you. All your faults, your fears, and your pettiness add a certain grace to your soul. I feel that I would detest a strong woman, a Sappho, courageous, full of energy and passion. Oh frail, gentle creature! How can you be otherwise? This angel's voice, this delicate voice, would have been against nature if it had come from a body other than yours."

'"I cannot give you any hope," she said. "Stop talking to me like that, because people would make fun of you. It is imposs-ible for me to forbid you to enter the theatre, but if you love me, and if you are sensible, you will not go there again. Listen to me, sir," she said in a serious voice.

'"Oh! Be quiet," said the artist, intoxicated, "the obstacles kindle the love in my heart." Zambinella retained a graceful and modest attitude, but she kept quiet, as if a terrible thought had revealed some misfortune to her.

'When it was necessary to return to Rome, she got up into a Berlin carriage,[54] ordering the sculptor, in an imperiously cruel manner, to return there alone by the phaeton. On the way Sarrasine resolved to abduct Zambinella. He spent the whole day occupied with making plans, each one more extravagant than the others.

'As night was falling, just as he went out to go and ask some people where the palace in which his mistress lived was situated, he met one of his friends in the doorway. "My dear friend," the latter said to him, "I have been asked by our ambassador to invite you to come to his house this evening. He is giving a magnificent concert, and when you learn that Zambinella will be there..."

'"Zambinella!" exclaimed Sarrasine, in a frenzy at the name. "I'm mad about her."

'"You are just like everyone else," his friend replied.

'"But if you are my friends, you, Vien, Lautherbourg and Allegrain,[55] then will you lend me your assistance after the festivities?" asked Sarrasine.

'"It doesn't involve killing a cardinal, not…"

'"No, no," said Sarrasine, "I ask nothing of you that decent people could not do."

'In a short time the sculptor arranged everything to ensure the success of his undertaking. He was one of the last to arrive at the ambassador's home, but he arrived there in a carriage harnessed to strong horses, led by one of the most enterprising *vetturini*[56] in Rome. As the ambassador's palace was full of people, it was not without difficulty that the sculptor, unknown to all those present, reached the drawing room, where at that moment Zambinella was singing.

'"It's doubtless out of consideration for the cardinals, the bishops and the priests, isn't it," asked Sarrasine, "that *she*[57] is dressed as a man, that she has her hair done up in a bag behind her head and combed back, and a sword at her side?"

'"She! Who's this 'she'?" replied the old lord whom Sarrasine was addressing.

'"Zambinella."

'"Zambinella?" continued the Roman prince. "You're joking. Where do you come from? Has a woman ever mounted the stage in the theatres of Rome? And don't you know by what kind of creatures the roles of women are performed in the Papal State? It is I, sir, who have endowed Zambinella with his[58] voice. I've paid for everything for that odd fellow, even for his singing master. Well, he feels so little gratitude for the service that I rendered him that he has never wanted to set foot in my house again. And yet, if he makes a fortune for himself, he will owe it all completely to me."

'Prince Chigi[59] could have doubtless gone on talking for a long time, but Sarrasine was not listening to him. An awful truth had penetrated into his soul. He had been struck as though by a bolt of lightning. He remained motionless, his eyes fastened on the sham singer. The blazing look on his face had a kind of magnetic influence on Zambinella, for the *musico*[60] finally looked away suddenly towards Sarrasine, and his heavenly voice wavered. He trembled. An involuntary murmur had escaped from the gathering, which he had a hold over as though it were attached to his lips, and it completely disconcerted him. He sat down, and interrupted his aria.

'Cardinal Cicognara, who had spotted in the corner of his eye the direction in which his protégé looked, then noticed the Frenchman. He leaned towards one of his ecclesiastical assistants, and appeared to ask the sculptor's name. When he had obtained the answer that he wanted, he looked at the artist very attentively, and gave orders to a priest, who disappeared promptly. However Zambinella, having recovered, started again the piece that he had interrupted in such an arbitrary way, but he performed it badly and refused, despite all the insistent demands made to him, to sing something else. It was the first time that he exerted this arbitrary tyranny, which later made him no less famous than his talent and his immense fortune, due, it is said, no less to his voice than to his beauty.

'"It's a woman," said Sarrasine, believing himself to be alone. "There's some secret plot behind it. Cardinal Cicognara is deceiving the Pope and the whole city of Rome!" Immediately the sculptor left the drawing room, gathered his friends together and prepared an ambush in the courtyard of the palace. When Zambinella had assured himself that Sarrasine had departed, he appeared to recover some calmness. Around midnight, after having wandered around drawing rooms like a man looking for his enemy, the *musico* left the gathering. Just as he was passing through the door of the palace, he was adroitly seized by some men, who gagged him with a handkerchief and put him in the carriage hired by Sarrasine. Frozen with horror,

Zambinella stayed in a corner without daring to make a movement. He saw before him the terrible face of the artist, who kept a deathly silence.

'The journey was short. Zambinella, abducted by Sarrasine, soon found himself in a dark, bare studio. The singer, half dead, remained on a chair, without daring to look at a statue of a woman, in which he recognised his own features. He did not utter a word, but his teeth chattered. He was paralysed with fear. Sarrasine strode around. Suddenly he stopped in front of Zambinella.

"Tell me the truth," he demanded in a muffled and wavering voice. "Are you a woman? Cardinal Cicognara…"

'Zambinella fell on his knees and replied only by lowering his head. "Ah! You are a woman," exclaimed the artist in a frenzy, "for even a…" He did not finish. "No," he continued, "*he*[61] would not be so despicable."

'"Ah! Don't kill me," exclaimed Zambinella, bursting into tears. "I only agreed to deceive you to please my friends, who wanted to have a laugh."

'"Laugh!" replied the sculptor in a voice that was like a diabolical roar. "Laugh, laugh! You dared to play with a man's passion?"

'"Oh! Have mercy!" replied Zambinella.

'"I ought to have you killed!" shouted Sarrasine, drawing his sword with a violent movement. "But," he continued with cold contempt, "by delving into your being with a dagger would I find any feeling there to extinguish, any revenge to satisfy? You are nothing. If you were a man or a woman I would kill you! But…" Sarrasine made a gesture of disgust, which forced him to turn his head, and so he looked at the statue. "And that is an illusion," he exclaimed. Then turning towards Zambinella: "A woman's heart was for me a refuge,

42

a homeland. Have you any sisters who resemble you? No. Well then, die! But no, you shall live. Letting you live, isn't that to doom you to something worse than death? It's not my own relatives or my own existence that I feel sorry for, but the future and the fate of my own heart. Your stupid action has spoilt my happiness. What hope can I rob you of for all those that you have caused to wither? You have brought me down to your level. *To love and be loved* are from now on words devoid of any meaning for me, as they are for you. I shall constantly think of that imaginary woman, when I see a real woman." He indicated the statue with a gesture of desperation. "I shall always have in my memory a divine harpy, who will come and stick her claws in all my masculine feelings, and who will stamp all other women with the mark of imperfection. You monster, who can give life to nothing, you have emptied the world of all its women." Sarrasine sat down in front of the terrified singer. Two large tears came from his dry eyes, rolled all the way down his male cheeks and fell to the ground: two tears of rage, two acrid and scalding tears. "No more love! I am dead to all pleasure, to all human emotions." With these words, he seized a hammer and hurled it at the statue with such excessive force that he missed it. He thought he had destroyed this monument to his folly, and so he took up his sword again and brandished it, to kill the singer. Zambinella emitted piercing cries. At that moment three men entered, and suddenly the sculptor fell down, pierced by three stiletto blows. "On behalf of Cardinal Cicognara," said one of them.

'"It is a kind deed, worthy of a Christian," replied the Frenchman as he breathed his last. These grim emissaries informed Zambinella of the anxiety of his protector, who was waiting at the door in a closed carriage, in order to be able to take him away as soon as he was freed.'

'But,' Mme de Rochefide said to me, 'what connection is there between this story and the little old man whom we saw at the de Lantys' home?'

'Madame, Cardinal Cicognara became the owner of the statue of Zambinella and had it made in marble. Today it is in the Albani Museum.[62] It is there that in 1791 the de Lanty family found it again and asked Vien to make a copy of it. The portrait that showed you Zambinella at twenty years old, just after having seen her as a centenarian,[63] served later as a model for Girodet's[64] *Endymion*. It was possible for you to recognise the Adonis type in it.'

'But is Zambinella a "he" or a "she"?[65]

'The only person who would know that, madame, is the great-uncle of Marianina. You must now be able to understand the interest that Madame de Lanty may have in hiding the source of a fortune that comes from…

'Enough!' she said, making an imperious gesture to me.

We remained plunged into profound silence for a moment.

'Well?' I said to her.

'Ah!' she exclaimed, getting up and striding about the room. She came and looked at me and said in a wavering voice: 'You have made me feel sick of life and its passions for a long time. Except in monsters, aren't all human feelings resolved in that way, by dreadful disappointments? Mothers and children kill us, whether it be through their bad behaviour or through their coldness. As wives we are betrayed. As lovers we are neglected and abandoned. Is there such a thing as friendship? Tomorrow I would become a devout person, if I did not know how to be able to remain strong like an inaccessible rock in the midst of the storms of life. If the Christian future is yet another illusion, at least it is only destroyed after death. Let me be alone.'

'Ah!' I said to her, 'You know how to punish someone.'

'Could I be wrong?'

'Yes,' I replied with a sort of courage. 'As a conclusion to this story, quite well known in Italy, I can give you a good idea of the progress made by modern civilisation. They don't make wretched creatures like that any more.'

'Paris,' she said, 'is a hospitable place. It welcomes all, both shameful fortunes and fortunes covered in blood. Crime and infamy have the right of refuge there, and encounter sympathy there. Virtue alone has no altar there. Yes, pure souls have a homeland in heaven. There will be nobody there who has known me! I am proud of that.'

And the marchioness remained pensive.

A Passion in the Desert

'This show is frightening!' she exclaimed as she came out of M. Martin's menagerie.[66]

She had just been looking at that daring speculator *working* with his hyena, to speak in the style used on posters.

'By what means,' she went on, 'can he tame his animals to the point of being sufficiently sure of their affection, to…'

'This fact, which seems to be problematic for you,' I replied, interrupting her, 'is however something quite natural…'

'Oh!' she exclaimed, letting an incredulous smile spread across her lips.

'Do you believe then that animals are entirely devoid of passions?' I asked her. 'Let me tell you that we can attribute to them all the vices that are due to our state of civilisation.'

She looked at me in amazement.

'But,' I continued, 'when I saw Monsieur Martin for the first time, I confess that I let out, as you did, an exclamation of surprise. I found myself then next to a former military man, whose right leg had been amputated and who had come in with me. The figure had struck me. He had one of those bold heads, branded by war and inscribed with Napoleon's battles. This old soldier had above all an air of frankness and cheerfulness, which always bodes favourably for me. He was doubtless one of those troopers who are surprised by nothing, who find something to laugh at in the last grimace of a friend, and bury him or gaily fleece him, who challenge cannonballs expertly, and, finally, who discuss things only briefly, and who would fraternise with the devil. After having looked very attentively at the owner of the menagerie just as he was coming out of the dressing room, my companion pursed his lips to express mocking contempt, with that kind of significant pout that superior men take the liberty of making to distinguish themselves from fools. Also, when I exclaimed about Monsieur

Martin's courage, he smiled, and said, with the air of an expert, shaking his head: "I've experienced it!..."

'"What do you mean 'experienced it'?" I replied. "If you would explain this mystery to me, I would be very much obliged to you."

'After a few moments, during which we got to know each other, we went to have dinner at the first restaurant with a display that caught our eye. During the dessert a bottle of champagne restored the memories of this strange soldier in all their clarity. He told me his story and I saw that he was justified in exclaiming "*I've experienced it!*"'

When we had returned to her home, she irritated me so much, and made so many promises, that I agreed to write down what the soldier had confided in me. So the following day she received this episode from a saga that could be entitled: *The French in Egypt*.

At the time of the expedition undertaken in Upper Egypt by General Desaix,[67] a Provençal soldier, having been overpowered by the Maghrebi,[68] was taken by these Arabs into the desert areas situated beyond the cataracts of the Nile. In order to put sufficient space between themselves and the French army for their own peace of mind, the Maghrebi undertook a forced march and did not stop till night. They camped around a well concealed by palm trees, near which they had previously buried some provisions. Not imagining that the idea of flight would occur to their prisoner, they were content to tie his hands together, and they all fell asleep after having eaten some dates and given some barley to their horses. When the bold Provençal man saw that his enemies were unable to keep watch on him, he used his teeth to get hold of a scimitar, and then, using his knees to hold its blade firmly, he cut the ropes that prevented him from using his arms, and he was free. At once he grabbed a rifle and a dagger, and took the precaution of acquiring a supply of dried dates, a small bag of barley, powder and bullets. He hung a scimitar around him, mounted a horse, and headed off swiftly in the direction in which he assumed that the French army must be.

Impatient to see a bivouac again, he drove the warhorse, which was already tired, so hard that the poor animal expired, its flanks torn, leaving the Frenchman in the middle of the desert. After having walked for some time in the sand with all the courage of an escaping convict, the soldier was forced to stop, as the day was coming to an end. In spite of the beauty of the sky during the night-time in the Orient, he did not feel he had the strength to continue on his way. Fortunately he had reached a hillock on the top of which there soared some palm trees, the foliage of which, having been visible for a long time, had awakened in his heart the sweetest hopes. His weariness was so great that he lay down on a granite rock, by chance shaped like a camp bed, and fell asleep without taking any precaution to defend himself while he was asleep. He had made the sacrifice of his life. His last thought was even a regret. He was already repenting having left the Maghrebi, whose wandering life was beginning to appeal to him, now that he was far away from them and helpless.

He was woken by the sun, whose merciless rays, falling straight down on the granite, created intolerable heat on it. Now the Provençal man had made the mistake of placing himself in the opposite direction to the shade cast by the majestic verdant crowns of the palm trees... He looked at those solitary trees and started! They reminded him of the elegant shafts crowned with long leaves that distinguish the Saracen[69] columns in the cathedral of Arles. But when, after having counted the palm trees, he cast a look around him, the most awful despair descended on his soul. He saw a boundless ocean. The blackish[70] sands of the desert stretched away as far as the eye could see in all directions, and they sparkled like a blade of steel struck by a bright light. He did not know if it was a sea of sheets of glass or lakes joined together like a mirror. Swept away in waves, a fiery vapour swirled around over that moving earth. The sky had an oriental brilliance of that purity that makes you despair, for it leaves nothing to be desired by the imagination. The sky and the earth were on fire. The silence was frightening in its wild and terrible majesty. Infinity, and a sense of the immensity of it all, pressed upon the soul from all sides: not a cloud in the sky, not a breath of air, nothing uneven in the sand moved by any small slight waves. Finally, the horizon terminated, as at sea when it is fine, in a line of light as slim as the sharp edge of a sword. The Provençal man hugged the trunk of one of the palm trees as if it had been the body of a friend. Then, in the shelter of the thin, straight shadow that the tree outlined on the granite, he wept, sat down and stayed there, contemplating with a profound sadness the harsh scene that presented itself to his eyes. He wept as though to test the solitude. His voice, lost in the cavities of the hillock, produced in the distance a thin sound, which did not stir up any echo at all. The echo was in his heart: the Provençal man was twenty-two years old, and he armed his rifle.

'There will always be time!' he said to himself, putting the liberating weapon on the ground.

Looking by turns at the blackish space and the blue space, the soldier was dreaming about France. He smelled with delight the gutters of Paris, he remembered the towns he had passed through, the faces of his friends, and the slightest details of his life. Finally, his southern imagination enabled him soon to make out the pebbles of his beloved Provence in the play of heat that moved in waves above the sheet stretched across the desert. Fearing all the dangers of this cruel mirage, he went down the opposite side of the hill to that which he had climbed the previous day. He felt great joy on discovering a kind of cave, carved out naturally in the immense fragments of granite that formed the base of this hillock. The remains of a mat revealed that this refuge had formerly been inhabited. Then a few feet away he noticed some palm trees loaded with dates. At that moment the instinct that makes us cling on to life awoke again in his heart. He hoped he could live long enough to wait for some Maghrebi to pass by, or perhaps he would soon hear the sound of cannons, for at that moment Bonaparte was overrunning Egypt. Revived by this thought, the Frenchman knocked down several bunches of ripe fruit, under the weight of which the date palms seemed to bend, and, as he enjoyed the taste of this unhoped-for manna, he felt sure that the inhabitant of the cave had cultivated the palm trees. The tasty fresh flesh of the dates indicated indeed the care taken by his predecessor. The Provençal man changed suddenly from being in dark despair to being almost mad with joy. He went back up to the top of the hillock and busied himself for the rest of the day with cutting down one of the infertile palm trees that had provided a roof for him the day before. A vague memory made him think of desert animals, and anticipating that they might come to drink at the remote spring amongst the sands that appeared at the base of the rocky areas, he resolved to safeguard himself against their visits by putting a barrier across the door of his hermitage. Despite his enthusiasm, despite the strength gained from the fear of being devoured while he was asleep, it was impossible for him to cut the palm tree into several pieces in the course of the day; but he succeeded in chopping it down. When, towards evening, this king of the desert fell, the noise of its fall resounded far away, and it was as though the solitude had let out a moan. The soldier shuddered at it as though he had heard some voice predict some misfortune for him. But, like an heir, who does not feel sorry for long at the death of a relative, he stripped this beautiful tree of the high, broad green leaves that decorate it poetically, and made use of them to repair the mat on which he was going to sleep. Tired by the heat and the work, he fell asleep under the red wall-coverings of his humid cave.

In the middle of the night his sleep was disturbed by an extraordinary sound. He sat up, and the deep silence that prevailed enabled him to recognise a different rhythm of breathing, the primitive force of which could not belong to a human being. A deep fear, increased more by the darkness, by the silence and by his waking fantasies chilled him to the heart. He could hardly even feel the painful contraction of his hair, when, by dilating the pupils of his eyes, he noticed in the darkness two pale yellow gleams. At first he attributed these lights to some reflection in his pupils, but soon, as the brilliance of the night helped him to distinguish gradually the objects which were in the cave, he could make out an enormous animal lying down two paces away from him. Was it a lion, a tiger or a crocodile? The Provençal man was not educated enough to know what subgenus his foe could be classified as, but his terror was all the more violent as his ignorance caused him to think about all these misfortunes together. He endured the cruel torture of listening to, of understanding, the variations in this breathing, without missing any of it, and without daring to allow himself the least movement. A smell as strong as that exhaled by foxes, but more penetrating, deeper, so to speak, filled the cave. And when the Provençal man had savoured it with his nose, his terror reached its height, for he could no longer doubt the existence of his terrible companion, whose royal den provided him with a bivouac. Soon the gleams of the moon, which, as it rushed towards the horizon, was illuminating the lair, gradually caused the speckled skin of a panther to shine brightly. This Egyptian lion was sleeping, curled up like a big dog, the calm owner of a sumptuous kennel at the door of a mansion; its eyes, open for a moment, had closed again. It had its face turned towards the Frenchman. A thousand confused thoughts passed through the mind of the panther's prisoner. At first he wanted to kill it with one shot from his gun, but he realised that there was not enough space between it and him to take aim at it. The gun would have missed the animal. And what if he woke it up? This hypothesis rendered him motionless. Hearing his heart beat in the midst of silence, he cursed those pulsations that were too strong and caused by the influx of blood, fearing he might disturb its sleep, which enabled him to try and find a beneficial solution. He put his hand twice on his scimitar with the intention of cutting off the head of his enemy, but the difficulty of cutting short stiff fur forced him to give up his daring plan. 'To fail? That would mean certain death,' he thought. He preferred taking his chances in a fight, and decided to wait till it was day. And he was not kept waiting long before it was daylight. So the Frenchman was able to examine the panther: its snout was stained with blood. 'It's eaten well!...' he thought, without concerning himself whether the feast had consisted of human flesh, 'so it won't be hungry when it wakes up.'

It was a female. The coat on her belly and haunches had a white sparkle. Several small patches similar to velvet formed pretty bracelets around her paws. The muscular tail was of the same whiteness but ended in black rings. The upper part of her dress, of a yellow like dull gold, but very smooth and soft, bore those characteristic flecks, subtly differentiated by their rose-shaped forms, that serve to distinguish panthers from other species of the felix family. This calm and peaceful hostess purred in a pose as graceful as that of a female cat lying on the cushion of an ottoman. Her bloody paws, sinewy and well-equipped, were in front of her head, which rested on them, and from which emerged those unique straight whiskers, similar to silver wires. If she had been like that in a cage, the Provençal man would certainly have admired the elegance of this animal and the strong contrasts of her vivid colours, which lent to her robe, like that of a magistrate, an imperial splendour. But at that moment he felt his vision disturbed by that sinister appearance. The presence of the panther, even asleep, caused him to experience the effect that the hypnotising[71] eyes of a snake are said to have on a nightingale. The soldier's courage finally evaporated for a moment in the face of this danger, while it would doubtless have been heightened in the mouths of cannons spewing out iron shot. However, a bold thought dawned on him, and dried up at its source the cold sweat that ran down from his forehead. Acting like those men who, driven to the end of their tether by misfortune, manage to defy death and face up to its blows, he saw, without realising it, a tragedy in this adventure, and resolved to play his role in it with honour till the last scene.

'The day before yesterday wouldn't the Arabs perhaps have killed me?...' he said to himself. Regarding himself as already a dead man, he awaited bravely and with an anxious curiosity the awakening of his enemy. When the sun appeared, the panther suddenly opened her eyes. Then she stretched out her paws violently, as though to loosen them up and get rid of cramps. Finally, she yawned, revealing thus the terrifying array of her teeth and her forked tongue, as rough as a grater. 'She's like a little mistress!' the Frenchman thought, seeing her roll over and make the most gentle and coquettish movements. She licked the blood that stained her paws and her snout, and scratched her head with repeated gestures full of gentleness. 'Fine!... Do your little bit of grooming!' the Frenchman said to himself, having found some cheerfulness again on regaining his courage, 'Let us greet each other.' And he seized the short little dagger which he had taken from the Maghrebi.

At that moment the panther turned her head towards the Frenchman and stared at him fixedly without moving forward. The rigidity of those metallic eyes and their unbearable clarity made the Provençal man start, especially when the animal walked towards him, but he looked at her in an affectionate way, and eyeing her as though trying to hypnotise her, he let her come close to him. Then, with a movement that was as gentle and amorous as if he had wanted to caress the prettiest woman, he passed his hand over her whole body, from head to tail, disturbing with his nails the flexible vertebrae that divided the yellow back of the panther. The animal raised her tail voluptuously, and her eyes became softer. And when, for the third time, the Frenchman performed this flattering act of self-interest, she let out one of those purring sounds by which our cats express their pleasure. But this murmur came from a gullet so powerful and so deep that it resounded in the cave like the last groans of an organ in a church. The Provençal man understood the importance of these caresses, and repeated them so as to put this imperious courtesan into a daze and stupefy her. When he felt certain of having subdued the ferocity of his capricious female companion, whose hunger had fortunately been satisfied the day before, he got up and was going to go out of the cave. The panther just let him go, but when he had climbed up the hillock, she leaped, with the lightness of a sparrow jumping from one branch to another, and came and rubbed herself against the soldier's legs, hunching her back like a cat. Then, looking at her host with eyes that had become less inflexible, she uttered that wild cry that naturalists compare to the sound of a saw.

'She's demanding!' exclaimed the Frenchman with a smile. He tried playing with her ears, stroking her belly and scratching her head firmly with his nails. And, perceiving his success, he tickled her head with the point of his dagger, looking out for a moment to kill her; but the firmness of her bones made him tremble, so that he could not manage to do it.

The sultana of the desert showed approval of the talents of her slave by raising her head, craning her neck, and showing up his exhilaration by the serenity of her attitude. The Frenchman thought suddenly that, in order to assassinate this shy princess with one blow, it was necessary to stab her in the throat, and he was raising the blade, when the panther, having eaten her fill no doubt, lay down gracefully at his feet, throwing him glances from time to time, in which, despite a hardness natural to her, there was also visible, confusingly, some benevolence. The poor Provençal man ate his dates, leaning against one of the palm trees, but from time to time he cast a glance at the desert, looking out for people who might liberate him, and at his terrifying companion, watching for any sign of uncertain leniency. The panther looked at the place where the date stones were falling, each time he threw one of them, and her eyes still had an expression of incredible wariness. She examined the Frenchman with business-like caution, but this examination was favourable to him, for when he had finished his meagre meal, she licked his shoes, and, with her strong, rough tongue, she miraculously removed the dust embedded in the creases.

'But when she feels hungry?...' thought the Provençal man. Despite the shudder that this idea caused him, the soldier, out of curiosity, started to measure the proportions of the panther, certainly one of the most beautiful individuals of her species, for she was three feet[72] high and four feet long, not including the tail. This powerful weapon, rounded like a cudgel, was almost three feet in length. The head, as large as that of a lioness, was distinguished by a rare keen expression: the cruelty of the tiger certainly dominated it, but there was also a vague resemblance to the appearance of a hypocritical woman. Finally the face of this solitary queen revealed at that moment a sort of gaiety similar to that of the drunken Nero: she had quenched her thirst in blood and wanted to play. The soldier tried coming and going and the panther let him move freely, content with following him with her eyes, resembling in this way less a faithful dog than a large angora goat, anxious about everything, even the movements of its master. When he turned round he noticed beside the spring the remains of his horse, the corpse of which the panther had dragged up there. About two thirds of it had been devoured. This sight reassured the Frenchman. It was now easy therefore for him to explain the absence of the panther, and the respect that she had had for him while he was asleep. This first bit of good luck made him take a bold risk with his future, and he conceived the mad hope of getting along with the panther all day long, not failing to try any means of taming her and gaining her good favours. He came back close to her and had the ineffable pleasure of seeing her wag her tail with an almost imperceptible movement. So he sat down without fear beside her, and the two of them started to play together. He took her paws, her snout, twisted her ears, turned her over on her back, and scratched firmly her hot silky flanks. She let him do it, and when the soldier tried to stroke the fur on her paws, she retracted her nails, hooked like Damascan swords.[73] The Frenchman, who kept one hand on his dagger, still thought about plunging it into the belly of the too trusting panther, but he was afraid of being immediately strangled in the last convulsion that might shake her. And what is more he sensed in his heart a sort of remorse, which cried out to him to respect a harmless creature. It seemed to him that he had found a female companion in this endless desert. He thought involuntarily about his first mistress, whom he had nicknamed *Mignonne*,[74] ironically, because during the whole time their passion lasted, he had to fear the knife, with which she had always threatened him. This memory of when he was young gave him the idea of trying to make the young panther, whose agility, gracefulness, and softness he now admired with less dread, answer to this name.

Towards the end of the day, he had familiarised himself with his dangerous situation and he was almost enjoying his feelings of anxiety. At last, his female companion finished by getting used to looking at him, when he called out in a falsetto voice '*Mignonne*'. When the sun went down, Mignonne uttered several times a deep melancholy cry.

'She's well brought up!...' thought the merry soldier. 'She's saying her prayers!...' But this witty thought did not occur to him until he had noticed the peaceful bearing that his female friend retained. 'Go on, my little blonde creature, I'll let you lie down first,' he said, relying very much on the movement of his own legs to escape as quickly as possible, when she had fallen asleep, in order to go and find another shelter during the night. The soldier waited impatiently for the time for his escape, and when it had arrived he walked vigorously in the direction of the Nile. But scarcely had he gone a quarter of a league in the sands than he heard the panther leaping along behind him, and uttering from time to time that saw-like cry, even more frightening than the heavy sound of those leaps.

'So!' he said to himself, 'she has developed some feeling of friendship for me!… This young panther has perhaps never met a human being. It is flattering to have one's first love.' At that moment the Frenchman fell into one of those areas of quicksand that are so dreadful for travellers, and from which it is impossible to save oneself. Feeling himself caught, he let out a cry of alarm, and the panther seized him by the collar with her teeth, and leaping back vigorously, she pulled him from the abyss, as if by magic. 'Ah! Mignonne,' exclaimed the soldier, caressing her enthusiastically, 'between us it's now till death us do part. But you're not just playing with me, are you?' And he retraced his steps.

From that moment on it was as though the desert were full of people. It contained a being to which the Frenchman could talk, and whose ferocity had become milder for his sake, without him being able to explain the reasons for this incredible friendship. However powerful the desire of the soldier was to stay on his feet and on his guard, he fell asleep.

When he woke up, he could not see Mignonne any more. He went up onto the hill, and in the distance he saw her leaping towards him, in the way that those animals usually do for whom running is not possible, due to the extreme flexibility of their spinal column. Mignonne arrived with bloody lips and received the essential caresses that her companion gave her, even showing by several deep purrs how much it pleased her. Her eyes full of gentleness turned, with even more mildness than the previous day, towards the Provençal man, who talked to her as though to a domestic pet.

'Ah! Ah! Young lady, you're a decent young girl, aren't you? You see? We do like to be cuddled. Don't you have any shame? Have you eaten a Maghrebi? Fine! They're animals like you though!… But don't go crunching Frenchmen at least… I wouldn't love you anymore!…'

She played as a young dog plays with its master, letting herself be rolled over, beaten and patted by turns, and sometimes she provoked the soldier by pushing forward her paw at him, in a soliciting gesture.

Several days passed in this way. Her company enabled the Provençal man to admire the sublime beauty of the desert. As soon as he had discovered there periods of fear and tranquillity, food, and a creature that was in his thoughts, his mind became troubled by contrasts… It was a world full of opposites. Solitude revealed to him all its secrets, wrapped him in its charms. He discovered in the rising and the setting of the sun sights unknown to the world. He learned to tremble on hearing above his head the gentle whistling sound of the wings of a bird – a rare traveller! – and on seeing the clouds merging together – changing coloured wanderers! He studied during the night the effects of the moon on the ocean of the sands, where the simoom produced waves and ripples and rapid changes. He lived according to the oriental day, and he admired its marvellous splendours, and often, after having enjoyed the tremendous sight of a hurricane on that plain, where the stirred-up sands produced red fogs and lethal dense clouds, he watched the night come with delight, for then the beneficent coolness of the stars would fall. He listened to pieces of imaginary music in the skies. Then solitude taught him how to display to himself the treasures of daydreaming.

He spent whole hours recalling trifles, in comparing his past life with his present life. Finally, he developed a passion for his panther, for he needed some affection. Whether his will, projected powerfully, had modified the character of his female companion, or whether it was because she could find abundant nourishment, thanks to the battles that were engaged in at that time in those deserts, she respected the life of the Frenchman, who finished by no longer being on his guard against her, seeing that she was so well tamed. He used the greater part of the time in sleeping, but he had to keep a look out like a spider at the centre of its web, so as not to let the moment of his deliverance escape him, should someone pass through the area defined by the horizon. He had sacrificed his shirt to make it into a flag flown from the top of a palm tree stripped of its foliage. Necessity taught him how to find a means of keeping it deployed by stretching it out with sticks, for the wind would not have been able to wave it at the moment when the expected traveller would be looking out into the desert...

It was during the long hours when hope abandoned him that he played with the panther. He had finally learned the different inflections of her voice, the expression in her looks, and he had studied the variations in all the marks that made slight differences in the gold of her robe. Mignonne did not even roar when he took hold of the tuft at the end of her formidable tail to count the black and white rings. It was a graceful ornament, which shone from afar in the sun like set stones. He took pleasure in contemplating the fine soft lines of her contours, the whiteness of her belly, the elegance of her head. But it was above all when she frisked about that he took pleasure in watching her, and the agility, the youthfulness of her movements always surprised him. He admired her suppleness when she started to leap, crawl along, creep, curl up, cling onto something, roll over, snuggle up or dash off all over the place. However quick she was in her enthusiasm, however slippery a block of granite was, she would stop short completely at the word *Mignonne*...

One day a huge bird hovered in the air. The Provençal man left his panther to examine this new guest, but after waiting for a moment, the abandoned sultana gave a muffled roar.

'I think, God preserve me, that she's jealous,' he exclaimed, seeing her eyes become hard again. 'The soul of Virginie[75] must have passed into that body, I'm sure!...' The eagle disappeared into the air while the soldier was admiring the rounded hindquarters of the panther. But there was so much elegance and youthfulness in her contours! She was as pretty as a woman. The blond fur of her robe blended its delicate tints with the matt white tones that distinguished the thighs. The abundant light of the sun made this vivid gold and the brown patches shine brightly in a way that made them indefinably attractive. The Provençal man and the panther looked at each other with a knowing air. The coquettish creature started when she felt the nails of her friend scratching her head. Both eyes flashed brilliantly, and then she closed them firmly.

'She has a soul...' he said, studying the serenity of this queen of the sands, gold like them, white like them, solitary and burning like them...

'Well,' she said to me, 'I have read your plea in favour of animals, but how did two persons so well suited to understand each other finish up?...'

'Ah! There you are! They finished as all great passions finish, with a misunderstanding. Each side believes the other

64

one has committed some kind of betrayal. One does not explain out of pride, and the other becomes confused out of stubbornness.'

'And sometimes, in the most beautiful moments,' she said, 'a look, an exclamation is enough. Well then, are you going to finish the story?'

'It's terribly difficult, but you will understand what the old soldier had already confided in me, when, while finishing his bottle of champagne, he exclaimed, "I don't know what wrong I had done her, but she turned round as if something had enraged her, and, with her sharp teeth, she cut into my thigh, only slightly, it's true. Thinking that she wanted to devour me, I plunged my dagger into her neck. She rolled over uttering a cry that froze my heart. I saw her struggling and looking at me without anger. For all the world, even for my cross,[76] which I did not yet have, I would have given her back her life. It was as though I had assassinated a real person. And the soldiers who had seen my flag and who ran to help me found me completely in tears."

'"Well, sir," he continued, after a moment's silence, "I've been around since the war, in Germany, Spain, Russia and France. I've taken this body of mine around a bit, and I haven't seen anything like the desert… Ah! That's really beautiful."

'"What do you feel about it?" I asked him. "Oh, that can't be said, young man. Besides, I still don't miss my bouquet of palm trees and my panther: I'd have to be a sad person to do that. In the desert, you see, there is everything and nothing."

'"But still, won't you explain it to me?"

'"Oh, well," he continued, letting slip a gesture of impatience, 'it's God without men.'"

NOTES

Sarrasine

1. Also known as Charles-Bernard Dugrail de la Villette (1805–50), talented novelist and friend of Balzac. He also, like the central character in the story, came originally from the region called Franche-Comté. The dedication dates from 1844 (see also note 22).

2. The name Lanty probably derives from the writings of Casanova (1725–98), but Lanti or Lante is also the name of a famous Roman family.

3. In the novel *La Maison du chat-qui-pelote*, Balzac created the character of the Duchess of Carigliano. Her husband, the Maréchal, is also referred to.

4. Monsieur de Nucingen and M. Gondreville are two characters who appear elsewhere in the *Comédie humaine*. Nucingen is a rich banker in *Le Père Goriot* and Gondreville is a statesman in *Une ténébreuse affaire*.

5. This refers to the famous story of Aladdin in *The Thousand and One Nights*.

6. Maria Malibran (1808–36) was a singer famous for her expression of emotions; Henriette Sontag (1808–54) was known for her pure and ethereal voice; Joséphine Mainvielle-Fodor was praised for the agility and ornamental qualities of her voice.

7. The anecdote about the Marquis de Jaucourt was included by Balzac in his anonymous collection *Album historique et anecdotique*.

8. Antinous was a young man of exquisite beauty who was a favourite of the Roman emperor Hadrian (AD 76–138).

9. Klemens Metternich (1773–1859), Austrian statesman.

10. Titus Flavius Vespasianus, known as Vespasian (AD 9–79). He was Roman emperor for the last nine years of his life. At one time he commanded the Roman army that occupied Britain. He is said to have coined the axiom 'Money has no smell'.

11. Mrs Anne Radcliffe (1764–1823), a British writer of sensational novels combining mystery and horror. Her most famous work is *The Mysteries of Udolpho*.

12. The original French is *Robin des Bois* (literally 'Robin of the Woods') and refers to the legendary Robin Hood, who features in the novel *Ivanhoe* by the novelist and poet Sir Walter Scott (1771–1832).

13. The Prince of Mysore could be either Haïder Ali (d. 1782) or his son Tippoo Sahib (1749–99), who were enemies of the British. Balzac probably found references to them in the writings of Sir Walter Scott (see also note 12).

14. The origin of this expression is obscure, but Genoa, in Italy, was the city in which the first merchant bankers appeared in the thirteenth century. The expression used by Balzac is doubtless an example of synecdoche, signifying someone who has obtained money through capitalist practices.

15. The French term *magnétiseur*, and the verb *magnétiser* (see note 71 to *A Passion in the Desert*), relate to the concept commonly discussed in the nineteenth century of 'animal magnetism', an attempt to understand the phenomenon of hypnosis, and also known as 'mesmerism' after the German doctor who developed the theory, Friedrich Anton Mesmer (1733–1815).

16. Joseph Balsamo Cagliostro (1743–95), an Italian doctor, who dabbled in the occult and was regarded as a charlatan.

17. The bailiff of Ferrette, Grand Prior of the Order of Malta, and long-time ambassador in Paris for the Grand Duke of Baden. He is referred to several times by Balzac in the course of the *Comédie humaine*.

18. The so-called Comte de Saint-Germain, who lived in France from 1750 to 1760 approximately, and is known to have died in 1784, claimed to possess the elixir of long life and asserted that he was several centuries old.

19. A gold coin worth twenty francs.

20. Antonio Gioacchino Rossini's (1792–1868) first opera, first performed in Venice in 1813 and in Paris in 1822. The cavatina referred to is that entitled '*Di tanti palpiti*', sung by the eponymous hero, a transvestite role, written for a woman but to be sung in a deep register.

21. Joseph Marie Vien (1716–1809), painter and sculptor, and director of the French Academy in Rome in 1775.

22. Franche-Comté is a region of France and an ancient province that comprised Haute-Saône, Doubs and Jura.

23. An ancient monetary unit. The word is also used to describe the British monetary unit 'pound', but this would be misleading here.

24. Form of address to members of the legal profession in France.

25. Sainte-Dié is in the Vosges area and has never been part of Franche-Comté.

26. Edmé Bouchardon (1698–1762), French sculptor.

27. Besançon is a town in the Doubs area of France (see also note 22).

28. The Marquis de Marigny (1727–81) was director-general of the king's buildings, arts and factories from 1751. He was the brother of Jeanne Antoinette Poisson, known as Madame de Pompadour (1721–64), a favourite of King Louis XV.

29. Denis Diderot (1713–84), French philosopher and editor of the *Dictionnaire Encyclopédique*.

30. Antonio Canova (1757–1822), influential Italian sculptor in the neoclassical style (see note 44).

31. The Comédie-Française is France's state theatre, with its own company of actors.

32. Madame Geoffrin held a literary salon frequented by the philosophers working on the *Dictionnaire Encyclopédique* (see also note 29).

33. There was a dancer with the name Clotilde at the Paris opera, but in 1793.

34. Sophie Arnould (1744–1803) was a singer who published several volumes of memoirs.

35. The full name of the theatre is the *Teatro di Torre Argentina*.

36. Niccolo Jomelli (1714–74) was a composer who was very popular early in his career but forgotten in the latter part of his life.

37. Balzac suddenly changes to using the present tense for these two verbs, but then returns immediately to using past tenses again.

38. Jean-Jacques Rousseau (1712–78), famous French philosopher, political writer and composer.

39. Baron Paul-Henri Holbach (1723–89) was a materialist and atheist who collaborated with Diderot on the *Dictionnaire Encyclopédique* (see note 29).

40. In French Balzac wrote '*de cet enfant*', meaning literally 'of this child', but the noun can be masculine or feminine, and so it was Balzac's choice to make it male. This is perhaps a significant detail in a story about ambiguous sexuality.

41. Pygmalion was a legendary sculptor from Cyprus who asked the goddess Aphrodite to provide him with a woman who looked like the statue he had fallen in the love with. The goddess brought the statue to life.

42. Santi Raphael (1483–1520) was a major Italian painter renowned for his portraits of women. Giorgio Barbarelli (1477–1510), known as Giorgione, was a member of the Venetian school and admired for his treatment of light.

43. Balzac translates the names of the buildings into French as *la rue du Corso* and *L'Hôtel d'Espagne*.

44. Count Cicognara (1767–1834), patriot and art historian, who a wrote a history of sculpture. He was the lover of the artist Antonio Canova (see note 30).

45. In French the possessive 'son' can mean 'his' or 'her' according to the context. This ambiguity becomes significant in the latter part of the story.

46. Poor little one (Italian).

47. Gentlemen and beautiful ladies (Italian).

48. Madame du Barry, born Jeanne Beçu (1743–93), became a countess by marriage. She was a famous writer and favourite of Louis XV.

49. Two strong Spanish wines.

50. To the infant, i.e. to Jesus Christ (Italian).

51. In the original French the name *Xérès* is used, which is a type of Spanish wine, also known as *Jerez*.

52. Frascati is a small town near Rome.

53. In the seventeenth century Cardinal Ludovisi had a magnificent villa with a large park constructed at Frascati. It no longer exists.

54. A covered, four-seater carriage, known in French as *une Berline* after the German city where it originated.

55. Jacques-Philippe de Lautherbourg (1742–1812), landscape painter; Christophe-Gabriel Allegrain (1710–95), sculptor.

56. Coachmen (Italian).

57. Emphasis Balzac's own.

58. As the truth about Zambinella's sexuality is revealed, the possessives *sa* and *son* must be translated as 'his' where relevant.

59. The Chigi are a famous Italian family.

60. In this context, *musico* means musical performer (Italian).

61. Emphasis Balzac's own.

62. In the eighteenth century Cardinal Albani had a magnificent villa built near Rome to house a collection of masterpieces of ancient statuary.

63. Balzac makes Zambinella a centenarian (*centenaire*), but he was twenty years old in 1758, so in 1830 he could only have been 92.

64. Anne Louis Girodet (1767–1824), a neoclassical artist who lived in Rome for five years, and a favourite artist of Balzac's.

65. In French, *Mais ce ou cette Zambinella?* The demonstrative adjectives can show gender in French.

A Passion in the Desert

66. Henri Martin opened his menagerie in December 1829. In 1881 he published *The Memoirs of a Tamer*.

67. General Louis Desaix de Veygoux (1768–1800) went with Napoleon to Egypt and conquered the Upper Nile.

68. Balzac's use of the name *Maghrebi* is geographically incorrect; the area known by Arabs as Maghreb is in North Africa. Some French writers used the term however to evoke vaguely oriental associations.

69. There are no 'Saracen columns' in the cathedral of Saint-Trophine in Arles. The use of the French adjective *sarrasin(e)* here and its use as the name of the eponymous sculptor in the story *Sarrasine* would appear to be coincidental.

70. In another version of the text, Balzac describes them as 'whitish'.

71. Balzac uses the verb *magnétiser* here, which refers to the belief in animal magnetism. See note 15 for *Sarrasine*.

72. Balzac uses the term *pied* (literally 'foot') here, which is an ancient unit of measurement equal to about 0.3248 of a metre.

73. A sword with a very fine steel blade, originally made in Damascus, Syria.

74. *Mignon(ne)* means sweet and kind (French).

75. It is not clear to whom this refers, as the name is not mentioned elsewhere in the story. It could be that the mistress referred to earlier by the nickname *Mignonne*, and after whom the soldier names the panther, is intended.

76. The cross of the Legion of Honour.

BIOGRAPHICAL NOTE

Honoré de Balzac was born in Tours in 1799. His father was a state prosecutor in Paris, but was transferred to Tours during the French Revolution due to his political opinions. The family returned to Paris in 1814.

Balzac spent his early years in foster care, and did not excel at school. He went on to study at the Collège de Vendôme and the Sorbonne, before taking up a position at a law office. In 1819 his family was forced to move from Paris for financial reasons. They settled in the small town of Villeparisis whereupon Balzac announced that he wanted to be a writer and returned to Paris. His early works, however, went largely unnoticed. In order to increase his reputation in the literary world, Balzac entered the publishing and printing business, but this enterprise was not a success and left him with heavy debts, which were to dog him for the rest of his life.

Dispirited, Balzac moved to Brittany in search of new inspiration, and in 1829 *Les Chouans* appeared. This was a historical novel in the style of Sir Walter Scott and marked the beginning of his recognition as a writer. Between 1830 and 1832 he published six novelettes entitled *Scènes de la vie privée*.

In 1833 he had the idea of linking together his existing writings to form one extensive work encompassing the whole of society. This led to the remarkable *Comédie humaine* – a work of some ninety-one novels, with a cast of in excess of 2,000 characters, providing a comprehensive image of the life, habits and customs of the French bourgeoisie. Among the most celebrated works of the *Comédie humaine* are *La Peau de chagrin* (1831), *Les Illusions perdues* (1837–43), *La Rabouilleuse* (1840) and *La Cousine Bette* (1846). Balzac spent fourteen to sixteen hours a day writing in order to fulfil his ambitious plans.

During the later years of his life, Balzac befriended Eveline Hanska, a rich Polish lady, through a series of letters, and then, in 1848, he travelled to Poland to meet her. Despite his failing health, the two were married in 1850, although their marriage was to prove short-lived as Balzac died only three months later, on 18th August, in Paris.

Dr David Carter, born in London in 1945, is a writer, translator and freelance journalist, and currently Professor of Communicative English at Yonsei University, Seoul. He has also taught at the universities of St Andrews and Southampton, in the UK, and has published on German and French literature, psychoanalysis, aesthetics, film history, drama and applied linguistics. His most recent books include *Georges Simenon* (2003), *Literary Theory* (2006), and he has translated Simenon's *Three Crimes* for Hesperus Press (2006).